God, Satan on Trial

By Jean Marie DIA

Universal Tribunal Court

TABLE OF CONTENTS:

Universal tribunal court has decided to take God, Satan to the court, for multiples reason: Genocide, Wars, Rape, Earthquakes (Natural disasters).

Where is God? Some have a hard time reconciling this disaster with God's goodness, while others divorce God from what they see as a natural disaster; God lets the victims grieve and lets disease spread and children suffer abuse.

The Author has been trying to figure out why God created natural disaster? Is God able to avoid Genocide, Rapes, Wars, and beheading people?

How a God who is powerfully, can be considered good and loving?

People look at the world around them and they see a lot wrong with it, Babies are born with birth defects, people are die tragically, natural disaster kill thousands of innocents, why does God create bad things?

Universal tribunal court charged God, Satan for crimes against humanity, non-assistance of person in danger.

Introduction:

Thank you friends for all assistance regarding of the publication of this book, Author take this opportunity explain to the world motivation and disappointment that most people had been victim and still victim, Author believe that God created this world, he believe that God is present all over the world, he believe that God know the past, present, and future, he believe that God is able to avoid any disasters, damages, wars, genocides, rapes, diseases.

Author still and still believe that Satan is a world "instigator "who excite people by committed most crimes, reference to Job (Bible): God told Satan to destroy Job live and he did what God told him. Author he is a father of five kids, two boys and 3 girls, author loves kids, Author believe that all parents had the right to protect their kids, social, education etc...

Author believe that most religious leaders play the role of hypocrite , all disasters committed by God; never complaint to God that God is wrong, for religious leaders, Satan is responsible of all crimes. This book explains that God is not able to assist person in danger, why? Who know?

REPUBLIC OF JUSTICE

IN AND UNIVERSAL TRIBUNAL COURT

UNIVERSAL TRIBUNAL COURT

VS.

GOD, SATAN, DEFENDANTS.

Presiding Judge: Jeremiah Marcus

Prosecutor: Samuel Fort

Defense lawyer (God) for the Defendant God: Boyd Babylon

Defense lawyer (Satan) for the Defendant Satan (Lucifer): Otto Atom

Jury:

Adolphine Schmorell

Kurt Fraser

Bernard London

Lecanard Bob

Hill Lumiere

Lebeau Gordon

Breitenlandenberg Paul

Lion Harvey

Anna Lecoeur

Pompidou Lesabre

Moise Colclough

Barzan Lungu.

Republic of Justice, charge God for Murders, Negligence, Conspiracy, Non-assistance of person in danger, crimes against humanity, Genocide.

Republic of Justice, filed accusation against Satan Lucifer for, destruction of live, complicity of murders, Architect of instigator of Genocides, wars, rapes, conspiracy.

Tribunal Penal universal

Mr. God, and Satan, you will be presumed innocent and the State must prove beyond a reasonable doubt you are guilty. Reasons will prove with justifications of innocents. You can testify or remain silent, the Jury will decide whether you are guilty or not and if you are found guilty or not, the Judge will sentence you.

Prior to the interrogation of a person suspected of crimes he/she must be told that he/she has the right to remain silent, the right to legal counsel. Nevertheless, the right to be told that anything he/she says; can be used in court against them. Furthermore, if the accused person confesses to the authorities the prosecution must prove to the Judge that the Defendant was informed of those above and knowingly waived those rights.

The Defendant has the right to a trial before a Jury. Jury's will be chosen and remain anonymous.

Ladies and Gentlemen of the Jury: It is my duty as Judge to instruct you in the law which applies to this case. It is your duty as Jurors to follow these instructions and to apply the rule of law stated in these instructions regardless of any opinion you may have as to what the law ought to be. It would be a violation of your oath to base a verdict upon any other view of the law than that give in the instructions of the court , in these instructions , any rule, direction or idea is repeated or stated in different ways , no emphasis thereon is intended by me and none may be inferred by you. For that reason, you are not to single out any certain sentence or any individual point or instruction and ignore the others, but you are to consider all the instruction as a whole and regard each in the light of all the others.

The order in which the instructions are given has no significance importance.

The evidence which you are to consider in this case consists of the testimony of the witnesses, the exhibits and any facts admitted or agreed to by counsel statements, arguments and opinions of counsel are not evidence in the case. However if the attorneys stipulate to the existence of a fact, you must accept the stipulation as evidence and regard that fact as proved.

You must not speculate to be true any insinuations suggested by a Question. Asked a Witness a question is not evidence and may be considered only as it, applies meaning to the answer, you must disregard any evidence to which an objection was sustained by the court and any evidence ordered stricken by the court, anything you may have seen or heard outside the courtroom is not evidence and must also be disregarded.

You must decide all questions of fact in this case from the evidence received in this trial and not from any other source.

The credibility or believability of witnesses should be determined by their manner upon the stand, their relationship to the parties, their fears, motives, interests or feelings, their opportunity to have observed the matter to which he or she testified the reasonableness of their statements and the strength or weakness of their recollections.

If you believe that a witness has lied about any material fact in this case, you may disregard the entire testimony of that witness or any portion of that testimony which is not proved by the other evidence.

Certain testimony has been read into evidence from a deposition, A deposition is testimony taken under oath before the trial and preserved in writing, you are to consider that testimony as if it had been given in court.

Judge:

Thank you Gentleman: today we open for the first time in this planet judgment against God and Satan, Thank you Mr. God and Satan to respond to this Court, We have plaintiffs from the Earth, who accepted to represented all Earth Continent, We have God Witnesses who may a have testify in God behalf, We have Satan present in this Court. I would like the prosecutor to open his argument and the reason for accusation against God, after we done with all procedures with God, and Satan will be the next for Judgment, Jury deliberation will be the last in the all procedures.

Silence? (Judge). Defendant God and Satan, criminal case is those in which a Defendant is accused of a serious crime, example murder. The prosecutor needs to prove that the defendant committed a crime; prosecutor is an attorney who represents the Republic of Justice, according to the law and the rules of court.

The juror's role is to hear the evidence presented by the prosecutor and the Defense attorney.

Evidence is presented to the jury by witnesses who testify, after all the evidence has been presented, the jury discusses in private. If all the jurors believe the evidence proves the defendant committed the crime, the jury convicts the defendant by returning a guilty verdict. After a defendant is convicted the judge imposes a sentence.

If the jurors do not believe the evidence proves the defendant committed the crime, then the jury acquits the defendant by returning a verdict of not guilty.

If the jurors are unable to decide between conviction and acquittal the Judge can declare a mistrial and a new trial can be held with different jurors.

Mr. God and Satan, In this particular case I will suggested to a plea bargain, If you agrees to plead guilty, the prosecutor can impose a sentence less severe, the plea bargain can be enter before or during the trial. It is important that people have confidence in the legal system, they will support it and their respect for the law will grow.

The goal of ours court is to provide equal of the planets, regardless of their wealth, position or physical disability.

Prosecutor

Thank you audience, thank you all plaintiffs, thank you Mr. God, thank you Mr. Satan Lucifer, thank you Defense lawyers. I'm the prosecutor for the State of Justice, after review all complaint by plaintiffs in the earth. I will read accusation against God, I will like permission to the Judge that Satan case will be try later.

Judge: Accepted

Prosecutor: Thank you Judge

Mr. God, the earth successful has file a complaint against you, you are accused of murder, genocide, earthquake, tornado, conspiracy , natural disasters, wars, non- assistant of person in danger, crimes against humanity

 Rape against children and women, the world has lost too many lives, we know that you were present; you know the past, present, and the future.

 You know the beginning and the end, you are everywhere, you are able to predict or to prevent all natural disasters, and you had all right to put the world in peace. You are able to install peace throughout the world, you are able to prevent all disease, peace, justice, you are the architect of the world, all the world have hope in you. You know how the world spend all theirs times thinking about you; most people in the world love you. Today the worlds have decided to take you before   Universal Tribunal Court, you are been accused for multiples charges', atrocity, ineffectiveness leadership. A sovereign who loves his people doesn't act like you, the world is victim of atrocity, you did nothing to protect your peoples, you pretend that one or the other day you will judge the world, people would be punished, good people will stay with you. Mr. God, you have destroyed the world, earth quake, which caused millions deaths, wars that have caused thousand deaths, rapes, women, children, people suffering, no foods.

Malnutrition had caused dead before thee, injustice non protection of people in danger, unable to help, religious followers beheaded in front of you , the religious assassinated in front of you , they kill children , terrorists committed thousand murders before you, incurable diseases, you are directly responsible, When? How the world may believe that you are a good leader? Most planets are at peace, except the earth, why? When you will make this planet a world of peace? People need peace, freedom , fear Still is all over, today's scientists is able to destroy the planet with nuclear bomb ,what is your reaction in this matter most religious leaders pretend that one day you will resolve the situation in the earth , how can you resolve this matter ? , you are the first to make the world harder than the criminals of the world, we will quote all references to all atrocities that you are involve, knowing all consequences that the earth had been victimize . I will stated all action that the earth continue to suffer and lists of all atrocities, complicity, Mr. God, the earth is very happy for you appearance in this court , people outside the court enjoy.

Prosecutor: Mr. God, the World (Earth) had been complaint about you long time ago, to day I have the opportunity to file accusation against you in this Court.

Freedom is the basis of Earth; freedom is the hope of the world.

Mr. God you created the earth and heaven and all forms of life, you created male and female

My accusation is basis of all crimes that you are direct responsible, murders, Earthquake, Snowstorm, Sandstorm, Wars, Rape, and Genocide. The Earth had lost much life because of you, non-protection of the person in danger. Do you known how many people spend time for praying? But you don't care? And still kill them without a notice, you fail to protect the earth, I have many plaintiffs who may testify against, Innocent victims of crimes that they didn't committed, failed to prevented crimes.

My recommendation to the jury, find you guilty of Murders and sentence you to death by hanging.

If you plead guilty before the Jury, I will request less sentence by order you to stop killing or stop kill, bringing back all death people, do you understand Mr. God?, We have many people in the earth, didn't deserve to be kill, do you known that?

God (Defense lawyer). Defense:

Thank you Judge, thank you the prosecutor and thank you all audience.

After hear all accusation against my client prosecutor fail to show behind a reasonable double that my client committed a crime in the earth, this accusation is base in speculation and no by preponderance evidence, Honorable Judge, this is my motion requesting the court to dismiss all accusation against my client God.

Judge: After review al l accusation and the motion of dismissal, the Court denied the motion.

Prosecutor: Honorable Judge, I will call the first plaintiff Mr. Luxe from the Earth.

Mr. Luxe : swear under oath

Thank you honorable Judge, and thank you Prosecutor, I'm very glad to see God for the first time in my life, I born in good family who believe in God, My Dad, my Mom was praying every days, I work very hard to help my family's , one day I decided to married, I received finance contribution from friends , through my marriage we have fours beautiful kids, two girls and two boys, one day we went to church conference, because of this Mr. God, we went we come back, door was open, when got inside, I saw my daughter laid down, bleeding, both kids were death. Mr. God I didn't know what to do, my life was going in wrong way, my question to you, why you didn't save my kids? What my kids did wrong, to be treated like that? You are the powerful God, I will suggest that you be sentenced to death, and you are a big problem in this planet. Thank you.

Prosecutor: Mr. God you hear?

Judge: Defense lawyer do you want to say something?

Defense: I just wait all plaintiff finish their complaint and I will respond in the last.

Next plaintiff: Mr. Fleuve Rouge

Thank you Judge. My name is Fleuve Rouge, I was a former senate to the earth, I was elected more than five times, never had a problem with population, went I pass away, I was received by Angel Gabriel, he drove me to Redfireburn, inside my bed was only scorpion, my pillow sneak, food very sad, I drink water only one time a month, one piece of beans a month. Mr. God what I do to be in this condition? Went my prison will be over? Do you forgive Mr. God? Please I beg you

Interruption by Angel Gabriel

Angel: Don't act that you are innocent, let me show you a video from the Earth.

Judge ordered video to be expose

Angel: Mr. Angel here I saw you request to the senator a peine capital yes or no? few months later they approved you request do you remember?, few months later they killed innocents people didn't committed the crimes, few years later DNA show that many people had been killed without commit a crime, you are a responsible of all innocents people, Honorable Judge I have nothing to say more than that.

Mr. Crocodile (Plaintiff, former president of Republic of Lumiere).

I'm very disappointed to you Mr. God, I received request to my population to build more than 4,000 houses for the orphan, take me twelve months building, After we started building the houses, Mr. God you surprise me with Earthquake, we lost seventy five percent of Population, death all over, houses, schools, hospitals, cars, everything destroys, what me thing you are normal God? What you thing people need to pray you again? What is in your mind? Are you normal? You are above all criminal in the Earth Mr. God, try one day to expose yourself in Earth, people would kill you Mr. God, why make you live in secret? Because you committed more crime Mr. God, my hope is that the court find you guilty, if they was not the law in this planet I would slap you in the face Mr. God. I'm very thankfully to meet you in person, and I will let the people in the Earth that you are a criminal more than all criminal in the earth Mr. God. Thank you, I'm done.

Mr. Tonneur (Plaintiff from Redfireburn).I was a president of the Republic of Sand Red, I was told by many of friend leaders of my Religion that killed and drink blood was the only solution to stay in power for ever, I was ordered my security to kill twelve people a week so I can drink the blood, and I ordered my security to kill more than half millions people because they have intension to overthrow my regime, final one days I was arrested and sentenced to death, my God you know I spend all my life praying you? After I pass away Angel escorted me in bud place, he make me sleep in the snow, no food, please Mr. God forgive me and send me back to the earth. I will never act stupide again. Thank God and thank you Judge for gives me the opportunity to meet God in person.

Ms. Moon (Plaintiff of the Earth).

My Son was murdered in his house, he sustained multiple stab wounds, a slit throat and a gunshot to the head, my brother Apple was charged with first degree murder for his death, he was convicted of first degree murder and sentenced to death, few years a lady   of his friend confessed he was the killer of my son, my brother was put to death. My brother was with a friend while they were in the room he was forced to do drugs, although he was shot in the head with a 12 shot pump by his friend. He was only 15. Why?

Mr. God why you didn't help my brother, knowing that he didn't committed the crime, do you thing I will pray you again? I hope that the Justice put you to death to. I'm done.

Mr. Soleil (plaintiff of the earth).

My sister Pall spending almost a year walking through the forest to reach the town to search for her siblings, Pall was 12 years old at the time, her family fled the territory of Limo, after attacks by Danagu rebels, the rebels killed at least 896 civilians and abducted more than 350 children (Both victim of the rape by rebels , Pall was wounded and admitted to hospital, along with thousands of civilians, she later fled the hospital for the bush. , when she fled, and she fell into the hand of the rebels, they killed is father, and mother, four of them survived. Mr. God why you don't intervene ?, All her hope was God may help, Father, Mother death, to day Pall she 16 years old, God do you think she need to pray you again? To someone does help?. I'm done.

Mr. Joker (Plaintiff of the Earth).

My complaint against God, Mr. God I will like to tell you, what make you failed to protected you faithfully people, here is one example: They was one King by the name "King Lion".

King Lion did not know what "God" was all about, but he become angry when a believe Panzama corrected him for the way he was living.

The King was also involved in homosexuality activity; he was especially interested in his court pages.

King Lion turned into resentment and hatred for Panzama and his Religion.

A few of the King ambitions officers fueled his fears with lies, Panzama was beheaded.

The persecution had begun, before it was over, a hundred people died.

Twenty –two of them would be declared Saints.

With the death of Panzama, Scorpate become the chief Religion teacher of the King's faith pages.

King Lion's face twisted in rage, it can't be true, he yelled at his adviser. It is true, your steward has baptized four more, all men under the age of twenty-five.

Don't the fear to die like their friend Panzama, who was killed for his disobedience? That's the strange thing answered the adviser, they've held even more strongly to their faith after his death.

More young men are attracted to the Religion than ever.

The King called in Mr. Scorpate, he asked him, if he had been teaching religion to another page, Scorpate said yes, the King grabbed his spear and flung it violently through the young man's throat then the King shouted that no one was permitted to leave his headquarters.

War drums beat throughout the night calling the executioners in a hidden room.

Mr. Scorpate secretly baptized ten more pages, one was Saint Corbeau a cheerful generous thirteen years old, he was the youngest of the group, and Saint Panzama had often protected Corbeau from the king's lust.

Most of the twenty two believes who have been proclaimed Saints were killed.

They were forced to walk thirty seven miles to the execution site after a few days in prison, they were thrown into a huge fire and burned alive, seventeen of them believes were royal pages, one of believe boys Peter; his own father was the executioner that day.

Mr. God to know your responsibility in these murders, what you didn't provided any assistance to you believes? Why? I'm done Judge.

Mr. Bonbon (Plaintiff of the Earth, former Judge).

Today Mr. God, I will like to explain how bad you are, yes you created the world and you destroy yourself what you did, we have many scientists in the Earth, but none of them had a power to do what you do. I will explain to you about earthquake:

An Earthquake is the result of sudden release of energy in the earth's crust that creates seismic waves.

The seismicity, Seismic or seismic activity of an area refers to the frequency, type and size of Earthquake experienced over a period of times, earthquake are measured using observation from seismometers, the moment Magnitude is the most common scale on which earthquake larger than approximately 5 are reported for the entire globe. The more numerous earthquakes smaller than magnitude 5 reported by national seismological observatories are measured mostly on the local magnitude scale, also referred to as the Richter scale. These two scales are numerically similar over their range of validity magnitude 3 or lower earthquakes are mostly almost imperceptible or weak and magnitude 7 and over potentially causes serious damage over larger area as depending on their depth.

The largest earthquake in historic times have been of magnitude slightly over 9, although there is no limit to the possible magnitude, the most recent large earthquake of magnitude 9.0 or large was a 9.0 magnitude earthquake in

Japan, intensity of shaking is measured on the modified metrically scale, the shallower an earthquake, the more damage to structures it causes all else being equal.

At the earth's surface, earthquake manifest themselves by shaking and sometimes displacement of the ground, when the epicenter of a large earthquake is located offshore, the seabed may be displaced sufficiently to cause a tsunami, earthquake can also trigger landslides and occasionally volcanic activity in its most general sense, the world earthquake is used to describe any seismic event whether natural earthquake are caused mostly by rupture of geological faults.

Mr. God you are a responsible of all earthquakes, include the damages, I just list to you same disasters of earthquakes in the earth.

In the morning of September 1, 1923, the earthquake devastated Tokyo, the port city of Yokohama, surrounding prefectures of Chiba, Kanagwa, and Shizuoka, and caused widespread damage throughout the Kanto region. The power and intensity of the earthquake is easy to underestimate, but the 1923 earthquake managed to move the 93-ton Great Buddha statue at Kamakura. The statue slid forward almost two feet. Causality estimates range from about 100.000 deaths, approximately 40.000 who went missing and were presumed dead.

Here is the list of earthquakes and tsunamis in the United States of America.

January 26, 1700, Washington, Oregon, California, fatalities unknown

November 18, 1755, Massachusetts, unknown fatalities.

December 16, 1811, Missouri, unknown fatalities.

January 9, 1857 California, unknown fatalities.

April 24, 1867 Kansas

April 2, 1868 Hawaii

October 21, 1868 California

December 14, 1872 Washington

August 31, 1886 South Carolina

April 18, 1906 California

September 27, 1909 Indiana

October 3, 1915 Nevada

June 29, 1925 California

August 16, 1931 Texas

March 10, 1933 California

May 18, 1940 California

December 20, 1940 New Hampshire

April 1, 1946 Alaska

May 6, 1946 Wisconsin

December 4, 1948 California

April 13, 1949 Washington

July 21, 1952 California

March 9, 1957 Alaska

July 9, 1958 Alaska

August 17, 1959 Montana, Wyoming

March 27, 1964 Alaska

February 4, 1965 Alaska

April 29, 1965 Washington

August 9, 1967 Colorado

November 9, 1968 Illinois

October 2, 1969 California

February 9, 1971 California

July 9, 1975 Minnesota

August 1, 1975 California

May 2, 1983 California

October 28, 1983 Idaho

April 24, 1984 California

October 1, 1987 California

October 17, 1989 California

April 25-26, 1992 California

June 28, 1992 California

March 25, 1993 Oregon

September 20, 1993 Oregon

January 17, 1994 California

April 14, 1995 Texas

May 2, 1996 Washington

September 25, 1998 Pennsylvania

October 16, 1999 California

February 28, 2001 Washington

November 3, 2002 Alaska

December 9, 2003 Virginia

December 22, 2003 California

September 10, 2006 Florida

October 15, 2006 Hawaii

October 30, 2007 California

December 19, 2007 Alaska

April 18, 2008 Illinois

July 29, 2008 California

January 9, 2010 California

February 10, 2010 Illinois

July 7, 2010 California

December 30, 2010 Indiana

August 22, 2011 Colorado

August 23, 2011 Virginia

September 2, 2011 Alaska

November 5, 2011 Oklahoma

October 16, 2012 Maine

May 24, 2013 California

List of Earthquakes in Algeria

May 1716 Algiers Province, 20.000 dead, thousands injured

March 2, 1825 Blida Province, 7.000 dead, thousands injured

November 16, 1869 Biskra Province 40 dead, dozens injured

August 6, 1947 Annaba Province 3 dead, hundreds injured

September 9, 1954 Chlef Province 1.250 dead, 3.000 injured

January 1, 1965 M'Sila Province 5.000 dead, 9.000 injured

October 27, 1985 Annaba Province 6 dead, dozens injured

October 29, 1989 Tipaza Province 30 dead, 10.261 injured

May 21, 2003 Boumerdes Province 2.266 dead

May 27, 2003, Algiers Province

List of earthquakes in Argentina

1692 Salta

1782 Mendoza earthquake

1817 Santiago del Estero earthquake

1826 Trancas earthquake

1844 Salta earthquake

1861 Mendoza earthquake

1863 Jujuy earthquake

1871 Oran earthquake

1874 Oran earthquake

1880 Tunuyan earthquake

1888 Rio de la Plata earthquake

1892 Recreo earthquake

1894 San Juan earthquake

1894 Catamarca earthquake

1899 Yacuiba earthquake

1903 Mendoza earthquake

1906 Tafi del Valle earthquake

1907 Tucuman earthquake

Mr. God Argentina lost more than a millions people, unknown missing, presumed dead

1908 Salta earthquake

1908 Cruz del Eje earthquake

1913 Tucuman earthquake

1917 Mendoza earthquake

1920 Mendoza earthquake

1927 Mendoza earthquake

1929 Mendoza earthquake

1929 Southern Mendoza earthquake

1930 La Poma earthquake

1931 El Naranjo earthquake

1933 Tucuman earthquake

1934 Sampacho earthquake

1936 San Luis earthquake

1941 San Juan earthquake

1944 San Juan earthquake

1947 Cordoba earthquake

1948 Salta earthquake

1949 Tierra del Fuego earthquake

1952 San Juan earthquake

1955 Villa Giardino earthquake

1957 Villa Castelli earthquake

1959 San Andres earthquake

1966 Belen earthquake

1966 Tartagal earthquake

1966 San Juan earthquake

1967 Mendoza earthquake

1968 Chaco earthquake

1972 San Juan earthquake

1973 Catamarca earthquake

1973 Salta earthquake

1974 Oran earthquake

1977 La Rioja earthquake

1978 San Juan earthquake

1981 Tucuman earthquake

1985 Mendoza earthquake

1992 Timbo Viejo earthquake

1993 San Juan earthquake

1993 San Francisco

1997 Santiago del Estero earthquake

2002 La Rioja earthquake

2004 Catamarca earthquake

2006 Mendoza earthquake

2009 Jujuy earthquake

2009 Ituizaingo earthquake

2009 Cordoza earthquake

2010 San Juan earthquake

2010 Salta earthquake

2011 Salta earthquake

2011 Santiago del Estero earthquake

Mr. God?

List of earthquakes in Australia:

28 October 1842, Newcastle, New South Wales, caused alarm in Newcastle, causing damage in Melbourne and surroundings.

In 17 September 1855 , Offshore, New South Wales, damage in Hunter street and Newcastle suburbs of the Hill and Wallsend

18 June 1868, Newcastle, New South Wales

29 August 1868, Eastern Highlands, felt throughout North-eastern Victoria, Gippsland, Albury and South Wales, caused damage

28 August 1883, Gayndah, Queensland, caused major damage

13 July 1884 Tasman Sea, Tasmania and Victoria

12 May 1885, Tasman Sea

2 July 1885, Cape Liptrap

15 November 1886, Yass, New South Wales

26 January 1892, Tasman Sea, this was the strongest quake in a sequence of hundreds in the Tasman Sea between 1883 and 1892

10 May 1897 Beachport –Robe, South Australia Severe damage

19 September 1902 Warooka, South Australia, unknown deaths attributed by the earthquake, extensive damage.

14 July 1903 Warmambool, Victoria

Effects and damage:

Many people lost their life, panic, shaking, burst water, cracks in some buildings, Mr. God you are responsible of all world disastrous, do you understand?, let me informed you about United States of America.

In 1964 Alaska earthquake:

Two types of tsunami were produced by this seduction zone earthquake. There was a tectonic tsunami tsunami produced additional an about twenty smaller and local tsunami. These smaller tsunamis were produced by submarine landslides and were responsible for the majority of the tsunami damage. Tsunami waves were noted in over 20 countries, including Peru, New Zealand, Papua New Guinea, Japan, and Antarctica.

The largest tsunami wave was recorded in Shoup Bay, Alaska, with a height of about 67 meters.

Death toll, damage and causalities:

Sources indicate that about 136 people died as a result of the earthquake, 15 died as a result of the earthquake itself, 106 died from the subsequent tsunami in Alaska, 5 died from the tsunami in Oregon, and 13 died from the tsunami in California. Property damage was estimated at about $311 million dollars.

Anchorage was heavily damaged, and parts of the city built on sandy bluffs overlying, suffered landslides damage, Railroad slid, destroying many acres of buildings and city blocks in downtown Anchorage.

Most coastal towns in the Prince William Sound, Kenai Peninsula, and Kodiak Island areas, especially the major ports of Seward, Whittier and Kodiak were heavily damaged by a combination of seismic activity, earthquake caused fires.

Near Cordova, the Million Dollar Bridge crossing the Copper River also collapsed.

1906 San Francisco earthquake:

375 deaths were reported, hundreds of fatalities in Chinatown went ignored and unrecorded, the total number of deaths is still uncertain today, and is estimated to be roughly 3,000 at minimum.

Most of the deaths concurrent in San Francisco itself, Between 227,000 and 300,000 people were left homeless, half of the population was evacuated fled across the Bay to Oakland and Berkely. The earthquake and fire left long standing and significant pressures on the development of California. Property losses from the disaster have been estimated to be more than 400 million.

The 1906 Centennial Commemorations was set up as a clearing –house for various centennial events commemorating the earthquake.

Property damages caused by earthquake:

2011 Tohoku earthquake, Japan, 235 billion

1995 Great Hanshin earthquake, China 75 billion

2010 Chile earthquake 15-30 billion

1994 Northridge earthquake, United States 20 billion

2012 Christchurch earthquake, New Zealand 12 billion

1989 Loma Prieta earthquake, United States 11 Billion

921 earthquakes, Taiwan 10 billion

1906 San Francisco earthquake, United States 9.5 Billion

January 23, 1556, Shanxi, China 820.000 deaths from earthquake

December 16, 1920 Ningxia, Gansu (China), estimated death toll in Shanxi, China 273.000

July 28, 1976 Hebei, China, 242,000 Deaths

May 21, 526 Antioch Turkey 240,000 deaths

December 26, 2004 Indian Ocean, 230.000 Deaths

October 11, 1138, Aleppo, Syria 230.000 Deaths

January 12, 2010, Haiti, half million estimated death toll.

Morning of September 1, 1923, varied accounts hold that the duration of the earthquake was between 4 and 10 minutes. The earthquake had an epicenter deep beneath Izu Oshima Island in Sagami Bay. It' devasted "Tokyo", the surrounding prefectures of Chiba, Kanangawa, and Shizuoka, and caused widespread damage throughout the Kanto region.

But the 1923 earthquake managed to move the 93-ton Great Buddha statue at Kamakura, Mr. God failed to protected Buddha statue, the statue slid forward almost two feet, causality estimates range from about 100,000 to 142,000 deaths, approximately 40,000 who went missing and were presumed dead.

December 31, 1703, Edo, Japan, 10,000 death toll

November 1, 1755, Lisbon, Portugal, 60,000 deaths.

Mr. God, you are the author of all natural disaster that causes widespread destruction lots of collateral damage or loss of life, brought about by forces other than the acts of human beings, earthquakes, flooding, Volcanic, eruption, landslide, hurricanes etc...

July, 1931, China floods 1,000, 000-4,000.000 Death toll

September 1887 Yellow River flood, China, 900,000 death toll

January 23, 1556, Shaanxi earthquake, China 830,000 death toll

July 28, 1976, Tangshan earthquake, China, 242,000 death toll

November 13, 1970, Bhola cyclone (East Pakistan), 500,000 death toll

April 29, 1991, Bangladesh, 138.000 death toll

1993, North American Storm Complex (United States), 318 death toll

Mr. God, I have a list of natural disasters and the numbers of the deaths:

October 8, 1871, united States, death toll 2,500, Peshtigo Fire, Wisconsin

August 3, 1936, Soviet Union, death 1,200 Kursha Fire

October 12, 1918, united States, death toll 453, Cloquet Fire, Minnesota

September1, 1894, Great Hinckley Fire, Minnesota, United States

September 5, 1881, Tumb Fire, Michigan, United States, death toll 282

July 29, 1916, Matheson Fire, Ontario, Canada, death toll 273

1997, Sumatra and Kalimantan Fires, Indonesia, death toll 240

1949, Landes region France, death toll 230

May 1987, Black Dragon Fire, China, death toll 213

February 7, 2009, Black Saturday Bushfires, Australia, death toll 173

Deadliest floods:

1931, 4,000,000 death toll, China floods

1887, 900,000 death toll,

1887, 900.000 death toll, Yellow River, China Flood

1975, 229.000 death toll, China failure of 62 dams, the largest of which was Banqiao Dam, result of Typhoon Nina).

1935, 145,000 death toll, China, Yangtze River Flood

1530, 100,000 death toll, Netherlands, St. felix's flood, storm surge

1911, 100,000 death toll, Yangtze River Flood China

1287, 50,000 death toll, St Lucia's flood, storm surge, Netherlands

1212, 60,000 death toll, North Sea Flood, storm surge, Netherlands

1219, 36,000 death toll, St Marcellus flood, storm surge, Netherlands

Deadliest heat waves:

2003, 70,000 death toll, Europe, (heat).

2010, 56,000 death toll, Russia (Heat)

1988, 10,000 death toll, United States heat

1980, 5,000 death toll, United States heat

2010, 1,718 death toll, Japanese heat wave

Deadliest lightning strikes:

1856, 4,000 death toll, Palace of the Grand Master Explosion, Rhodes Greece

1769, 3,000 death toll, Church of San Nazaro Explosion, Brescia, Italy.

Deadliest blizzards:

1972, Iran Blizzard, death toll 4.000

1719, Carolean death march, Sweden/Norway, death toll 3.000

2008, Afghanistan blizzard, death toll 926

1888, Great blizzard (United States) death toll 400

1993, North American Storm Complex (United States) death toll 318

1888, Schoolhouse blizzard (United States) death toll 235

1902, Hakko-da Mountains incident, Japan, death toll 199

1996, North American blizzard (United States) death toll 154

1940, Armistice Day blizzard (United States) death toll 144

2008, Chinese winter storms, death toll 133

Deadliest tropical cyclones:

November 13, 1970, Bhola cyclone, East Pakistan (now Bangladesh) death toll 500.000

November 25, 1839, India cyclone, death toll 300.000

October 7, 1737, Calcutta cyclone, India, death toll 300.000

August 7, 1975, Super Typhoon Nina- contributed to Banqiao Dam failure, death toll 229.000

October 30, 1876, Great Backerganj Cyclone of 1876 (India, now Bangladesh) death toll 200.000

October 8, 1881, Haiphong Typhoon, Vietnam, death toll 300.000

April 29, 1991, Bangladesh Cyclone, death toll 138.866

May 2, 2008, Cyclone Nargis, Myanmar, death toll 138,366

1882, Bombay Cyclone, India, death toll 100.000

October, 1874, Bengal Cyclone India, death toll 80.000

Mr. God, here is most natural disasters committed by you in the earth

Mount Nyirangongo is an active stratovolcano with an elevation of 3470 m(11382 ft) in the Virunga Mountains associated with the Albertine Rift. It is located inside Virunga National Park, in the Democratic Republic of the Congo, about 20km(12mi) north of the town of Goma and lake Kivu and just west of the border with Rwanda. The main crater is about two kilometers wide and usually contains a lava lake.

Volcano in Africa(Demovratic Republic of Congo- Mount Nyiragongo).

Since 1882, it has erupted at least 34 times, including many periods where activity was continuous for years at a time, often in the form of a churning lava lake in the crater.

The volcano partly overlaps with two older volcanoes, Baratu and Shaheru, and is also surrounded by hundreds of small volcanic cinder comes from flank eruptions.

Volcanism at Nyirangongo is caused by Mr. God, were two parts of the African Plate are breaking apart.

The lava emitted in eruptions at Nyiragongo is often unusually fluid.

Nyiragongo's lavas are made of milliliter nephelinite, an alkali-rich type of volcanic rock whose unusual chemical composition may be a factor in the unusual fluidity of the lavas there.

Where's most lava flows move rather slowly and rarely pose a danger to human life.

Between 1894 and 1977 the crater contained an active lava lake. On 10 January 1977, the crater walls fractured, and the lava drained in less than an hour. The lava flowed down the flanks of the volcano at speeds of up to 60 miles per hour on the upper slopes, overwhelming villages and killing at least 120 people. The hazards posed by eruptions and consiprancy of Mr. God are unique to the earth.

Nowhere else in the world does such a steep-sided stratovolcano contain a lake of such fluid lava.

Nyiragongo's proximity to heavily populated areas increases its potential for causing a natural disaster that Mr. God created.

The 1977 eruption raised awareness of the unique dangers posed by Nyiragongo, and because of this was designated a decade Volcano, worthy of particular study, in 1991.

The eruption was preceded by the creation of a new small volcano, Murara, a short distance away on the slopes of Nyamuragira.

2002 eruption:

Lava lakes reformed in the crater in eruptions in 1982-1983 and 1994. Another major eruption of the volcano began on January 17, 2002, after several months of increased seismic and fumarolic activity. A 13 km fissure opened in the south flank of the volcano, spreading in a few hours from 2800 m to 1550 m elevation, reaching the outskirts of the city of Goma the provincial capital on the Northern shore of lake Kivu. Lava streamed from three spatter cones at the end of the fissures and flowed in a stream 200 to 1000 m wide and up to 2m deep through Goma.

Warning had been given and 400.000 people were evacuated from the city across the Rwandan border into neighboring Gisenyi during the eruption.

Lava covered the northern end of the runway at Goma International Airport, leaving the southern two-thirds usable, and surface, releasing lethally large amounts of carbon dioxide and methane, similar to the disaster at Lake Nyos in Cameroon in 1986.

About 147 people died in the eruption from asphyxiation by carbon dioxide and buildings collapsing due to the lava and earthquakes. At least 15% of Goma comprising 4,500 buildings were destroyed, leaving about 120.000 homeless.

Immediately after the eruption stopped, a large number of earthquakes were felt around Goma and Gisenyi. This swarm activity continued for about three months and caused the collapse of more buildings.

Six months after the start of the 2002 eruption, Nyiragongo erupted again. Activity at Nyiragongo is ongoing, but currently confined to the crater, where another lava lake has formed about 259 meters below the level of the 1994 lava lake.

Prosecutor: Mr. God, you complicity is the basis that the state of Necturne accused you for crimes that people on the earth had been victims and continue to be victims, ineffectiveness of leaderships, conspiracy of numerous murders, without any justification, We believe that your are the only leader of the earth, why make you thing that the world need to suffering because of you behalf stupidity, let me explain you about Natural disaster:

A natural disaster is a major adverse event resulting from natural processes of the Earth; examples include floods, volcanic eruptions, earthquakes, tsunamis, and other geologic processes.

A natural disaster can cause loss of life or property damage, and typically leaves some economic damage in its wake, the severity of which depends on the affected population's resilience, or ability to recover.

In 2012, there were 905 natural catastrophes worldwide, 93% of which were weather-related disasters. Overall costs were US $ 170 billion and insured losses $70 billion.

2012 was a moderate year, 45% were meteorological (storms), 36% were hydrological (floods), 12% were climatological (heat waves, cold waves, droughts, wildfires) and 7% were geophysical events (earthquakes and volcanic eruptions), between 1980 and 2011 geophysical events accounts for 14% of all natural catastrophes.

Cyclonic Storms:

Cyclone, tropical cyclone, hurricane, and typhoon are different names for the same phenomenon a cyclone that forms over the oceans. The deadliest hurricane ever was the 1970 Bhola cyclone; the deadliest Atlantic hurricane was the great Hurricanes of 1780 which devastated Martinique, St. Eustatius and Barbados, Another notable hurricane Katrina which devastated the Gulf Coast of the United States in 2005.

Extra tropical cyclones:

Extra tropical cyclones, sometimes called mid-latitude cyclones, are a group of cyclones defined as synoptic scale low pressure weather systems that occur in the middle latitude of the Earth(outside the tropics) not having tropical characteristics, and are connected with fronts and horizontal gradients in temperature and dew point otherwise known as "bar clinic zones". As with tropical cyclones, they are known by different names in different regions (North East, Pacific Northwest windstorms, European windstorm, East Asian-northwest Pacific storms, Sudestada and Australian east society, such as the storm surge of the North Sea flood of 1953 which killed 2251 in the Netherlands and eastern England, the Great Storm of 1987 which devastated southern England and France and the Columbus Day Storm of 1962 which struck the Pacific northwest.

Droughts:

A drought is unusual dryness of soil, resulting in crop failure and shortage of water for other uses, caused by significantly lower rainfall than average over a prolonged period. Hot dry winds, high temperatures and consequent evaporation of moisture from the ground can contributed to conditions of drought.

Well known historical droughts include:

In 1900 India killing 2500.000 to 3.25 million.

In 1921 Soviet Union in which over 5 million perished from starvation due to drought, Mr. God what you reaction for those murders?

1920-30, Northwest China resulting in over 3 million deaths by famine.

1936 and 1941 Sichuan Province China resulting in 5 million and 2.5 million deaths respectively.

1997-2009 Millennium Drought in Australian led to a water supply crisis across much of the country. As a result many desalination plants were built for the first time.

2006, Sichuan Province China experienced its worst drought in modern times with nearly 8 million people and over 7 million cattle facing water shortages.

12-years drought that was devastating southwest Western Australia, southeast South Australia, Victoria and Northern Tasmania was very severe and without historical precedent.

2011, the State of Texas lived under a drought emergency declaration for the entire calendar year. The drought caused the Bastrop fires.

Hailstorms:

Hailstorms are falls of rain drops that arrive as ice, rather than melting before they hit the ground.

A particularly damaging hailstorm hit Munich, Germany, on July 12, 1984, causing about 2 billion dollars in insurance claims.

Heat waves:

A heat wave is a period of unusually and excessively hot weather. The worst heat wave in recent history was the European heat Wave of 2003.

A summer heat wave in Victoria, Australia, created conditions which fuelled the massive bushfires in 2009. Melbourne experienced three days in a row of temperatures exceeding 40*C (104*F) with some regional areas sweltering through much higher temperatures. The bushfires, collectively known as Black Saturday, were partly the act of arsonists.

The 2010 Northern Hemisphere summer resulted in severe heat waves, which killed over 2,000 people.

It resulted in hundreds of wildfires which causing widespread air pollution, and burned thousands of square miles of forest.

Heat waves can occur in the ocean as well as on land with significant effects.

A tornado is a violent, dangerous, rotating column of air that is in contact with both the surface of the earth and a cumulonimbus cloud or, in rare cases, the base of a cumulus cloud. It is also referred to as a twister or a cyclone, although the word cyclone is used in meteorology in a wider sense, to refer to any closed low pressure circulation.

Tornadoes come in many shapes and sizes, but are typically in the form of a visible condensation funnel, whose narrow end touches the earth and is often encircled by a cloud of debris and dust.

Most tornadoes have wind speeds less than 110 miles per hour (117 km/h), are approximately 250 feet (80m) across, and travel a few miles before dissipating.

The most extreme tornadoes can attain wind speeds of more than 300 mph, stretch more than two miles across, and stay on the ground for dozens of miles.

The tri-State,Tornado of 1925, which killed over 600 people in the United States.

The Daulatpur Astoria Tornado of 1989, which killed roughly 1,300 people in Bangladesh.

Wildfires:

Wildfires are large fires which often start in wild land areas; common causes include lightning and drought.

Notable cases of wildfires were the 1871 Peshtigo Fire in the United States, which killed at least 1700 people, and the 2009 Victorian bushfires in Australia.

Natural disaster created by Mr. God

The 2004 Indian Ocean earthquake, the third largest earthquake recorded in history, registering a moment magnitude of 9.1-9.3, the huge tsunamis triggered by this earthquake killed at least 229.000 people

The 2011 Tohoku earthquake and tsunami registered a moment magnitude of 9.0. The death toll from the earthquake and tsunami registered a moment magnitude of 9.0. The death toll from the earthquake and tsunami is over 13.000, and over 12.000 people are still missing.

The 8.8 magnitude February 27,2010 Chile earthquake and tsunami cost 525 lives.

The 7.9 magnitude May 12,2008 Sichuan earthquake in Sichuan Province, China. Death toll at over 61,150 as May 27,2008

The 7.7 magnitude July 2006 Java earthquake, which also triggered tsunamis.

The 6.9 magnitude 2005 Azad Jammu& Kashmir and KPK province Earthquake, which killed or injured above 75.000 people in Pakistan.

Volcanoes can cause widespread destruction and consequent disaster in several ways. The effects include the volcanic eruption itself that may cause harm following the explosion of the volcano or the fall rock.

Second, lava may be produced during the eruption of a volcano. As it leaves the volcano, the lava destroys many buildings and plants it encounters. Third, volcano ash generally meaning the cooled ash-may form a cloud, and settle thickly in nearby locations.

When mixed with water this forms a concrete-like material.

In sufficient quantity ash may cause roofs to collapse under its weight but even small quantities will arm humans if inhaled.

Since the ash has the consistency of ground glass it causes abrasion damage to moving parts such as engines. The main killed of humans in the immediate surroundings of a volcanic eruption is the pyroclastic flows, which consist of a cloud of hot volcanic ash which builds up in the air above the volcano and rushes down the slopes when the eruption no longer supports the lifting of the gases. It is believed that Pompeii was destroyed by a pyroclastic flow.

A lahar is a volcanic mudflow or landslide. The 1953 Tangiwai disaster was caused by lahar, as was the 1985 Armero tragedy in which the town of Armero was buried and an estimated 23,000 people were killed.

A specific type of volcano is the super volcano. According to the Toba catastrophe theory 75,000 to 80,000 years ago a super volcanic event at Lake Toba reduced the human population to 10,000 or even 1,000 breeding pairs creating a bottleneck in human evolution. It also killed three quarters of all plant life in the northern hemisphere.

The main danger from a super volcano is the immense cloud of ash which has a disastrous global effect on climate and temperature for many years.

Mr. God master of floods disasters:

A flood is an overflow of an expanse of water that submerges land. The EU Floods directive defines a flood as a temporary covering by water of land not normally covered by water. In the sense of flowing water, the word may also be applied to the inflow of the tide. Flooding may result from the volume of water within a body of water, such as a river or lake, which overflows or breaks levees, with the result that some of the water escapes its usual boundaries. While the size of a lake or other body of water will vary with seasonal changes in precipitation and snow melt, it is not a significant flood unless the water covers land used by man like a village, city or other inhabited area, roads, expanses of farmland.

The John storm Flood of 1889 where over 2200 people lost their lives when the south Fork Dam holding back Lake Conemaugh broke.

The Huang He (Yellow River) in China Floods particularly often. The Great Flood of 1931 caused between 800,000 and 4,000,000 deaths.

The Great Floods of 1993 was one of the most costly floods in United States history.

The North Sea Flood of 1993 which killed 2251 people in the Netherland and eastern England

The 1998 Yangtze River Floods, in China, left 14 million people homeless.

The 2000 Mozambique flood covered much of the country for three weeks, resulting in thousands of deaths, and leaving the country devastated for years afterward.

The 2005 Mumbai floods which killed 1094 people.

The 2010 Pakistan Floods directly affected about 20 million people, mostly by displacement, destruction of crops, infrastructure, property and livelihood, with a death toll of close to 2,000.

Tropical cyclones can result in extensive flooding and storm surge, as happened with:

Bhola Cyclone, which struck East Pakistan(Now Bangladesh) in 1970

Typhoon Nina, which struck New Orleans, Louisiana in 2005

Limnic eruptions:

A limnic eruption occurs when a gas, usually CO_2, suddenly erupts from deep lake water, posing the threat of suffocating wildlife, livestock and humans. Such an eruption may also cause tsunamis in the lake as the rising gas displaces water. Scientists believe landslides, volcanic activity, or explosions can trigger such an eruption. To date, only two limnic eruptions have been observed and recorded:

In 1984, In Cameroon, a limnic eruption in Lake MO noun caused the deaths of 37 nearby residents.

At nearby Lake Nyos in 1986 a much larger eruption killed between 1,700 and 1,800 people by asphyxiation.

Tsunami can be caused by undersea earthquake as the one caused by the 2004 Indian Ocean Earthquake, or by landslides such as the one which occurred at Lituya Bay, Alaska.

Mr. God, Your area been charge for numerous crimes, Failure to protected the earth, Ineffectiveness of leadership, here is the lists of wars and death toll in the earth, you known and you should have known the consequence of you negligence:

Here is a list of wars and the consequences that you Mr. God created in the earth:

Millions of people died as a result of Mao Zedong's reforms, with most of these deaths being allegedly due to human rights abuses and administration errors within China. The total includes those who died during the Campaign to Suppress Counterrevolutionaries, the Three-anti and Five-anti Campaigns, human rights abuses in Tibet, The Great Leap Forward (especially the resulting famine),And the Cultural Revolution.

In 1949 to 1976 death toll in China, 78,000,000

Mass murders perpetrated by the Communist leaders of the Soviet Republics between 1917 and 1922 and later on in the Soviet Union during a period of 1922-1953(until death of Joseph Stalin), It included terror unleashed by Cheka during the Russian Civil War against nations and enemies of the revolution, deaths in Gulags, forced resettlements of the NKVD.

In 1917-1953, death toll 61,000,000 Soviet Union

Private forces under the control of Leopold II of Belgium carried out mass murders, mutilations, and other crimes against the Congolese in order to encourage the gathering of valuable raw materials, principally rubber. Significant deaths also occurred due to major disease outbreaks and starvation, caused by population displacement and poor treatment. Estimates of the death toll vary considerably because of the lack of a formal census before 1924, but a commonly cited figure of 10 million deaths was obtained be estimating a 50% decline in the total population during the Congo Free State and Appling it to the total population of 10 million in 1924.

Crimes during Congo Free State 1885-1908, death toll, 22,000,000

Sanctions imposed by the United Nations Security Council caused excess deaths of young children, death toll 576,000. Between 1990-1998

Massacres of people connected to the Indonesian Communist Party (PKI) were carried out in 1965 and 1966, death toll 2,000,000

War in the Vendee (France 1793-1796), described as genocide by some historians, death toll 250,000,000

During the Bosnia War, at least 100,000 people were killed 1992-1995

During the Battle of Manila, at least 100,000 civilians were killed (19445).

Civilian deaths under the Indonesian occupation of East Timor, including killings, disappearances, and deaths caused by conflict-related hunger and illness, death toll 202,600 (1974-1999).

A complain of political repression by right-wing dictatorships in South America, sponsored by the United States, Operation Condor, death toll 80,000, 1975-1983

The Nanking Massacre, commonly known as the Rape of Nanking, was a war crime committed by the Japanese militaries in Nanjing, then capital of the Republic of China, after it fell to the Imperial Japanese Army on 13 December 1937, Death toll 350,000

The sack of the second city of the Byzantine Empire by a Muslim fleet under the command of Leo of Tripoli, In addition to the thousands killed the Saracens fled also took 20,000 Greek slaves., Death toll 15,000, In 904 Byzantine Empire

Fires set during attacks on Greeks and Armenians by Turkish mobs and military forces in Smyrna at the end of the Greco-Turkish War (1919-1922). The violence and fires resulted in the destruction of the Greek and Armenian portions of the city and the evacuation of their former populations by British and American militaries forces. After the attacks 30,000 Greek and Armenian men left behind were deported by Turkish forces, many of whom were subsequently killed, Death toll 100,000 (1922).

At least 9,000 people were tortured and killed in Argentina from 1976 to 1983, carried out primarily by the Argentinean military Junta (part of Operation Condor), Death toll 30,000, Dirty War 1976-1983

With around 6 million Jews murdered as well as the genocide of the Romani : most estimates of Romani deaths are in the 200,000, but some estimate more than a million. A broader definition includes political and religious dissenters, 200,000 people with disabilities, 2 to 3 million Soviet POW, 5,000 Jehovah's Witnesses, 15,000 homosexuals and small numbers of mixed-race children (knwon as the Rhineland bastards), and millions of Polish and Soviet civilians, bringing the death toll to around 17 million.

Holodomor was a famine in Ukraine caused by the government of Joseph Stalin, a part of Soviet famine of 1932-1933. Holodomor is claimed by contemporary Ukrainian government to be a genocide of the Ukrainians. As of March 2008, Ukraine and nineteen other governments have recognized the actions of the Soviet government as an act of genocide. The joint statement at the United Nations in 2003 has defined the famine as the result of cruel actions and policies of the totalitarian regime that caused the deaths of millions of Ukrainians, Russians, Kazkhs and other nationalities in the USSRS. On 23 October

2008 the European Parliament adopted a resolution that recognized the Holodomor as a crime against humanity.

Some historians such as David Stanmard and Howard Zinn consider the deaths caused by disease, displacement, and conquest of Native American populations during European settlement of North and South America as Constituting an act of genocide. The alleged genocidal aspect aspects of this event are entwined with loss of life caused by the lack of immunity of Native Americans to diseases carried by European settlers.

Some estimates indicate case fatality rates of 80-90% in Native American populations during smallpox epidemics.

According to Noble David Cook, there were too few Spaniards to have killed the millions who were reported to have died in the first century after Old and New World contact.

On January 12, 2010, the Court of appeals in Kiev opened hearings into the fact of genocide-famine Holodomor in Ukraine in 1932-33, in May 2009 the Security Service of Ukraine had started a criminal case "in relation to the genocide in Ukraine in 1932-33, In a ruling on January 13, 2010 the court found Stalin and other Bolshevik leaders guilty of genocide against the Ukrainians.

Since the independence of Nigeria in 1960 the 3 ethnic groups, the Hausa, Yoruba, and Igbo, had always been fighting over control in the political realm. The Igbos seemed to have control over most of Nigeria's politics until the assassination of the then Igbo. PresidentJohnson Aguyi-Ironsi by Northern general Yakubu Gowon. With this the Igbos secedes from Nigeria and created the Republic of Biafra. The Igbos had the upper hand until late 1967 when food supplies were cut off. Igbos were starving and thousands more were being slaughtered by Nigerian soldiers. In 1970 the Igbo's surrendered to the Nigerians and by then anywhere from 1 to 3 million Igbos had either starved or had been killed.

Cambodian Genocide, 1975-1979, Death toll 3,000.000

Historian Charles Pete Banner Haley notes that slavery was not intentionally genocidal and resulted in the creation of a New World Afro-American" African slaves died in large numbers during transportation from Africa. The number could be more accurate if it included deaths during the acquisition of slaves in Africa and subsequent deaths in America. Before the 16th century the principal market for the warring African tribes that enslaved each other's populations was the Islamic world to the east. Gustav Nachtigal , an eye – witness, believed that for every slave who arrived at a market three or four died on the way.

Rwandan genocide, 1994, Death toll 1.000.00

Expulsion of Germans after World War II, 1945-1950, with at least 12 million Germans directly involved, it was the largest movement or transfer of any single ethnic population in modern history and largest among the post-war expulsions in Central and Eastern Europe (which displaced more than twenty million people in total). The events have been usually classified as population transfer, or as ethnic cleansing, Death toll 3,000.000

The expulsions as genocide, Felix Ermacora writing in 1991, considered ethnic cleansing to be genocide and stated that the expulsion of the Sudeten Germans was genocide..

Armenian Genocide, 1915-1923, usually called the first Genocide of the 20th century, despite recognition by some twenty one countries as genocide, Turkey disputes genocide by the Ottoman Empire. Death toll 1,500,000

Greek genocide, 1915-1923, death toll 1,000,000

Massacres of Poles by the Ukrainian insurgent Army, 1943-1944, systematically massacres by the Ukrainian Insurgent Army on Polish civilians in the eastern part of the Polish Second Republic, the victim's toll includes women, children and elderly people. The small minority of dead belong to different ethnic group (mostly Ukrainians protecting Polish peoples against assaults, but also Jews and Russians). Most of the victims were tortured prior to their death Disputed by Ukrainians, but considered genocide by the Polish authorities.

Bangladesh genocide, 1971, Atrocities in East Pakistani Armed Forces, leading to the Bangladesh liberation War and Indo-Pakistani War of 1971, are widely regarded as a genocide against Bengali people especially Crimes Tribunal in order to prosecute members of the Islamist Bangladesh Jamaat-e-Islami who were allegedly complicit in the genocide.

Mr. God, most religious leaders in the earth , believe that you are a loving father, able to protected the earth, through all accusation you still incapable to protect the earth, here is the list of the victims in prisons.

Deadly prisons and camps:

Auschwitz-Birkenau, run by Nazi Germany, 1940-1945, location Oswiecim,Poland, death toll 800,000

Treblinka, 1942-1943, death toll 700,000

Belzec, 1942-1943, death toll 600,000

Majdanek, 1942-1943, death toll 350,000

Chelmmo 1941-1943, death toll 300,000

Sobitor 1942-1943, death toll 260,000

Kolyma Gulag, run by Soviet Union (Kolyma location), death toll 150,000, 1932-1954

Bergen-Belsen , run by Nazi Germany, death toll 100,000 1942-1945

Neuengamme, run by Nazi Germany (hamburg) death toll 55,000 1938-1945

Jasenovac, run by Nazi Germany (Croatia) death toll 1941-1945

Jadovno, run by Nazi Germany, death toll 35,000 (1941).

Stara Gradiska, run by Nazi Germany, death toll 75,000, 1941-1945

Tuol Sleng, Democratic Kampouchea, location Cambodia, death toll 17,000, 1975-1979

Camp Sumter, Confederate States of America, location Andersonville, Georgia, USA, 1864-1865, death toll 13,171

Crveni Krst, Nazi regime, Nedic's Serbia, 1941, death toll 12,000

Gakovo, Yugoslavia, 1944, death toll 12,000

Omarska, Bosnia Serb forces, 1944, death toll 12,000

Tammisaari prison camp, Finland, 1918, death toll 3,000

Elmira Prison, United States of America, New York, 1864-1865, death toll 2,963

Rab , run by Italy, location Rab Croatia, death toll 2,000

Krugersdorp, United Kingdom, location Krugersdorp, Transvaal
Republic,1900-1902, death toll 1,800

Mr. God, the earth had lost many religious members, some had been
behead, torture etc, why? When are you being able to protect them?

Religious War:

The European wars of religion of the 16th and 17th centuries are the classical
example, often referred to simply as the wars of religion. Earlier wars also
frequently cited as religious wars, include the Muslim conquests (7th to 19th)
and the Christian militaries excursions against the Muslim conquests,
including the crusades (11th to 13 centuries).

The Spanish Reconquista (8th to 15 centuries) and the Ottoman wars in
Europe (15th to 19th centuries).

In more recent times, since the mid-20th century, violent conflicts along
religious lines have frequently been conflated with ethnic issues; examples
would include the Israel-Palestinian conflict, the Insurgency in the North
Caucasus, the Nagorno-Karabakh War, the Yugoslav Wars, the Second
Sudanese Civil War, the Syrian civil war or the Nigerian Sharia conflict, among
others. Other ongoing conflicts are predominantly motivated by religious
extremism i.e. involving a faction representing radical Islamic Jihadist, among
others those in Afghanistan and North –West Pakistan, Iraq, the Maghreb,
Yemen, Somalia, and the genocides and assimilation of the First Nations in
North America.

The European war against Muslim expansion was recognized as a religious
war. The early modern wars the Ottoman Empire were seen as a seamless
continuation of this conflict by contemporaries. The term religious war was
used to describe, controversially at the time, what are now known as the
European wars of religion, and especially the then-ongoing Seven Years War,
from at least the mid-18th century.

It is evident that religion as one aspect of a people's cultural heritage may
serve as a cultural marker or ideological rationalization for a conflict that has
deeper ethnic and cultural differences. This has been specifically argued for
the case of the troubles in Northern Ireland, often portrayed as a religious

conflict of a Catholic vs. a Protestant faction, while the more fundamental cause of the conflict was in fact ethnic rather than religious in nature. This conflict caused many people lost their life, and Mr. God failed to protected or bring peace.

Muslim conquest of the Indian subcontinent, from 1000 to 1525, death toll 80,000,000

World War II, Worldwide, 1939-1945, casualties and Second Sino-Japanese War, this include Holocaust and concentration camps deaths.

Mongol conquests, Eurasia, death toll 30,000,000 (1206-1368).

Late Yuan warfare and transition, China, 1340-1368, death toll 30,000,000

Qing dynasty conquest of the Ming Dynasty, China, 1616-1662, death toll 25,000,000

Taiping Rebellion (China) 1851-1864, death toll 100,000,000

World War I, includes worldwide Spanish flu deaths, Death toll, 65,000,000 (1914-1918).

Conquest of Timur-e-lang, West Asia, South Asia, Central Asia, Russia (1369-1405), death toll 20,000,000

A Lushan Rebellion (China) 755-763, death toll 36,000,000

Dungan revolt (China) 1862-1877, death toll 12,000,000

Conquest by the Empire of Japan, 1894-1945, death toll 30,000,000

Russian Civil War, 1917-1921, death toll 9,000,000

Congo War (Second) Democratic Republic of the Congo, 1998-2003, death toll 5,400,000

Napoleomic Wars, Europe, Atlantic, Pacific and Indian Ocean, 1803-1815, death toll 7,000,000

Holy War Roman Empire, 1618-1648 (Religious War) death tolls 11,500,000

Yellow Turban Rebellion (China) 184-205, death toll 7,000,000

Nigerian Civil War, 1967-1970 (Genocides in history of ineffectiveness of Mr. God), death toll 3,000,000

War in Afghanistan, 1979 to present, Soviet-Afghan War, Taliban and Nato intervention, death toll 2,000,000 or more

Polish-lithuanian Commonwealth, 1655-1660, death toll (Deluge) 4,000,000

Korean Peninsula, 1950-1953, death toll 4,500,000 (Korean War)

Vietnam War (Southeast Asia, 1955-1975), death toll 3,000,000

French Wars of Religion (France, 1562-1598), death toll 4,000,000

Shaka's conquests (Africa, 1816-1828), death toll 2,000,000

Sudan Civil War (Second War, 1983-2005), death toll 2,000,000

Crusades, Holy Land Europe (1095-1291) death toll 3,000,000, Religious War

Gallic Wars (France, 58bc, Roman Empire) death toll 1,000,000

Du Wenxiu Rebellion (China, 1856-1873) death toll 1,000,000

Mexican Revolution (Pancho Villa and Columbus Raid, 1911-1920) death toll 2,000,000

Iran-Iraq War (1980-1988) death toll 2,000,000

United States, Confederate States (American Civil War, 1861-1865), death toll 800,000

Spanish Civil War (Spain, 1936-1939), death toll 1,000,000

Paraguan War (South America, 1864-1870), death toll 1,200,000

In the Jewish religion, the expression Milkhemet (Hebrew, commandment war) refers to a war that is both sides obligatory for all Jews (Men and women) and limited to territory within the borders of the land of Israel. The geographical limits of Israel and conflicts with surrounding nations are detailed in the Tanakh, the Hebrew Bible, especially in Numbers 34-1-15 and Ezekiel 47-13-20

The Israel –Palestinian conflict can be viewed as an ethnic conflict, yet elements on both sides view it as a religious war as well. In 1929, religious tensions over the Wailing Wall led to the 1929 riots, including the Hebron and Safe massacres.

In 1947, the UN decided on partitioning the Mandate of Palestine, which led to the creation of the State of Israel, since then region has been plagued with conflict.

The 1948 Palestinian exodus also known as the Nakha (Arabic) occurred when approximately 726,000 Palestinian Arabs fled or were expelled from their homes, during the 1948 Arab-Israel War and the Civil War that preceded it. The exact causes remain the subject of fundamental disagreement between Palestinians and Israelis.

Jews makes a religious and historical claim to the land and Palestinians make historic claims to the land, So What You Mr. God think to resolve this conflict?

Pakistan and India, the all India league (AIML) was formed in Dhaka in 1906 by Muslims who were suspicious of the Hindu-majority Indian National Congress. They complained that Muslim members did not have the same rights as Hindu members.

A numbers of different scenarios were proposed at various times. Among the first to make the demand for a separate state was the writer/philosopher Allama Igbal, who, in his presidential address to the 1930 convention of the Muslim league said that a separate nation for Muslims was essential in an otherwise Hindu-dominated subcontinent, all conflicts caused live lost.

The Ethiopian –Adal war was a military conflict between the Ethiopian Empire and the Adal Sultanate from 1529 until 1559. The Imam Ahmad Ibn Ibrihim al-Ghazi came close to extinguishing the ancient realm of Ethiopia, and converting all of its subjects to Islam, the intervention of the European Cristovao da Gama, son of the famous navigator Vasco da Gama, helped to prevent this outcome. However, both polities exhausted their resources and manpower in the conflict, allowing the northward migration OF THE Oromo INTO THEIR PRESENT HOMELANDS TO THE NORTH AND West OF Addis Ababa. Many historians trace the origins of hostility between Somalia and Ethiopia to this war. Some historians also argue that this conflict proved, through their use on both sided, the value of firearms such as the matchlock musket, cannons, and the harquebus over traditional weapons.

Nigerian conflict, inter-ethnic in Nigeria has generally had a religious element. Riots against Igbo in 1953 and in the 1960 in the north were said to have been sparked by religious conflict. The riots against Igbo in the north in 1966 were said to have been inspired by radio reports of mistreatment of Muslims in the south. A military coup d'état led by lower and middle-ranking officers, some of them Igbo, overthrew the NPC-NCNC dominated government. Prime Minister Balewa along with other northern and western government officials was assassinated during the coup. The coup was considered an Igbo plot to overthrow the northern dominated government. A counter-coup was launched by mostly northern troops. Between June and July there was a mass exodus of Ibo from the north and west. Over 1.3 million Ibo fled the neighboring regions in order to escape persecution as anti-Ibo riots increased.

In the 1980s, serious outbreaks between Christians and Muslims occurred in Kafanchan in southern Kaduna State in a border area between the two religions.

The 2010 Jos riots saw clashes between Muslim herders against Christian farmers near the volatile city of Jos, resulting in hundreds of casualties. Officials estimated that 500 people were massacred in night-time raids by rampaging Muslim gangs.

Buddhist uprising: during the rule of the Catholic NgoDinh Diem, the discrimination against the majority Buddhist population generated the growth of Buddhist institutions as they sought to participate in national politics and gain better treatment. The Buddhist uprising of 1966 was a period of civil and military unrest in South Vietnam, largely focused in the I corps area in the north of the country in central Vietnam.

In a country where the Buddhist majority was estimated to be between 70 and 90 percent, Diem ruled with a strong religious bias. As a member of the

Catholic Vietnamese minority, he pursued pro-Catholic policies that antagonized many Buddhists.

Chinese conflict, the Dungan revolt (1862-1877) and Panthay Rebellion (1856-1873) by the Hui were also set off by racial antagonism and class warfare, rather than the mistaken assumption that it was all due to Islam that the rebellions broke out. During the Dungan, revolt fighting broke out between Uighurs and Hui.

In 1936, after Sheng Shicai expelled 20,000 Kazakhs from Xinjiang to Qinghai, the Hui led by General Ma Bufang massacred their fellow Muslims, the Kazakhs, until there were only 135 of them left.

Tensions with Uyghur's and Hui arose because Qing and Republican Chinese authorities used Hui troops and officials to dominate the Uyghur's and crush Uyghur revolts.

Xinjiang's Hui population has increased by over 520 percent between 1940 and 1982, an average annual growth rate of 4.4 percent, while the Uyghur population only grew by 1.7 percent. This dramatic increase in the Hui population led inevitably to significant tensions the Hui and Uyghur Muslim populations. Some old Uyghurs in Kashgar remember that the Hui army at the Battle of Kashgar (1934) massacred 2,000 to 8,000 Uyghurs, which caused tension as more Hui moved into Kashgar from other parts of China.

Some Hui criticize Uyghur separatism, and generally do not want to get involved in conflicts in other countries over Islam for fear of being perceived as radical Hui and Uyghur live apart from each other, praying separately and attending different mosques.

Lebanese Civil War: there is no consensus among scholars on what triggered the Lebanese Civil War. However, the militarization of the Palestinian refugee population, with the arrival of the PLO guerrilla forces did spark an arms race amongst the different Lebanese political factions. However the conflict played out along three religious lines, Sunni Muslim, Christian Lebanese and Shiite Muslim

It has been argued that the antecedents of the war can be traced back to the conflicts and political compromises reached after the end of Lebanon's administration by the Ottoman Empire. The Cold War had a powerful disintegrated effect on Lebanon, which was closely linked to the polarization that preceded the 1958 political crisis. During the 1948 Arab-Israel War an exodus of Palestinian refugees who fled the fighting or were expelled from their homes, arrived in Lebanon. Palestinians came to play a very important role in future Lebanese civil conflict, whilst the establishment of Israel radically changed the local environment in which Lebanon found itself.

Lebanon was promised independence and on 22 November 1943 it was achieved. French troops, who had invaded Lebanon in 1941 to rid Beirut of the Vicky forces, left the country in 1946. The Christians assumed power over the country and economy. A confessional parliament was created, where Muslims and Christians were given quotas of seats in parliament. As well, the President was to be a Christian, the Prime Minister a Sunni Muslim and the Speaker of Parliament a Shia Muslim.

In March 1991, parliament passed an amnesty law that pardoned all political crimes prior to its enactment. The amnesty was not extended to crimes perpetrated against foreign diplomats or certain crimes referred by the cabinet to the Higher Judicial Council. In May 1991, the militias were dissolved, and the Lebanese Armed Forces began to slowly rebuild themselves as Lebanon's only major non-sectarian institution. Some violence still occurred.

In late December 1991 a car bomb (estimated to carry 220 pounds of TNT) exploded in the Muslim neighborhood of Basta. At least thirty people were killed, and 120 wounded, including former Prime Minister Shafik Wazzan, who was riding in a bulletproof car.

Mr. God, do you known is you responsibility to avoid all crimes, and all disasters?

Here, we have causalities of the Syrian Civil War:

Estimates of deaths in the Syrian War, per opposition activist groups, vary between 150,000 (July 2013), the United Nations put out an estimate of over 100,000 that had died in the war.

Unicef reported that over 500 children had been killed, Mr. God no protection for the kids to? What people think you are a lovingly father, why?

Another 400 children have been reportedly arrested and tortured in Syrian prisons. Both claims have been contested by the Syrian government. Additionally, over 600 detainees and political prisoners have died under torture.

You fellow believe you are a loving father, loving leader, here is the list of Holy War, that you are a direct responsible of the atrocities committed with people that you support or support you.

Those who fought in the name of God were recognized as the Milites Christi, warriors or knights of Christ. The Crusades were a series of militaries campaigns that took place during the 11th through 13th centuries against the Muslim Conquests. Originally, the goal was to recapture Jerusalem and the Holy land from the Muslims, and support the besieged Christian Byzantine Empire against the Muslim Seljuk expansion into Asia Minor and Europe proper. Later, Crusades were launched against other targets, either for religious reasons, such as the Albigensian Crusade, the Northern Crusades, or because of political conflict, such as the Aragonese Crusade. In 1095, at the Council of Clermont, Pope Urban II raised the level of war from bellum lustrum (just war), to bellum sacrum (Holy war?). In 16th Century France there was a succession of wars between Roman Catholics and Protestants, known as the French Wars of Religion. In the first half of the 17th century, the German states, Scandinavia (Sweden) and Poland were beset by religious warfare in the Thirty Years War. Roman Catholicism and Protestantism figured in the opposing sided of this conflict, though Catholic France did take the side of the Protestants but purely for political reasons.

The Battle of las Navas de Tolosa, known in Arab history as the Battle of Al-Uqab, took place on 16, July 1212 and was an important turning point in the Reconquista and in the medieval history of Spain.

The forces of King Alfonso VIII of Castile were joined by the armies of his Christian rivals, Sancho VII of Navarre, Pedro II of Aragon and Alfonso II of Portugal in battle against the Berber Muslim Almohad rules of the southern half of the Iberian Peninsula.

Islam: Muslim conquests:

The Muslim conquests were a military expansion on an unprecedented scale, beginning in the lifetime of Muhammad and spanning the centuries, down to the Ottoman wars in Europe, and arguably continuing to the present day in the Sahel and in Darfur. Until the 13th century, the Muslim conquests were those of a less coherent empire, the Caliphate, but after the Mongol invasions, expansion continued on all fronts for another half millennium until the final collapse of the Mughal Empire in the east and the Ottoman Empire in the west with the onset of the modern period.

There were a number of periods of infighting among Muslims, there are known by the term Fitna and mostly concern the early period of Islam, from the 7th to 11th centuries, i.e. before the collapse of the Caliphate and the emergence of the various later Islamic empires.

While technically, the millennium of Muslim conquests could be classified as religious war, the applicability of the term has been questioned. The reason is that the very notion of a religious war as opposed to a secular wares the result of the Western concept of the separation of Church and State. No such division has ever existed in the Islam world, and consequently there cannot be a real division between wars that are religious from such that are non-religious. Islam does not have any normative of pacifism, and warfare has been integral part of Islam history both for the defense and the spread of the faith since the time of Muhammad. This was formalized in the juristic definition of war in Islam, which continues to hold normative power in contemporary Islam, inextricably linking political.

Mr. God, I'm very third of you leadership, you create many diseases, known that people will lost life, why you never be involve physically by protecting the earth, The earth and all world religious leaders, campaigning that you are a Merci, loving, anything they need you will assist them , how will mention same natural diseases that you are a responsible .

Black Death: was one of the most devastating in human history, resulting in the deaths of an estimated 75 to 200 million people and peaking in Europe in the years 1348-50. Although there were several competing theories as to the etiology of the Black Death, analysis of DNA from victims in northern and south Europe published in 2010 and 2010 indicates that the pathogen responsible was the "Yersinia pestis" bacterium, probably causing several forms of plague.

The Black Death is though to have originated in the arid plains of central Asia, where it then travelled along the Silk Road, reaching the Crimea by 1346. From there, it was most likely carried by Oriental rat fleas living on the black rats that were regular passengers on merchant ships. Spreading throughout the Mediterranean and Europe, the Black Death is estimated to have killed 30-60% of Europe's total population. All in all, the plague reduced the world population from an estimated 450 million down to 350-375 million in the 14th century.

The aftermath of the plague created a series of religious, social, and economic upheavals, which had profound effects on the course of European history. It took 150 years for Europe's population to recover occasionally in Europe until the 19th century.

Population history of the indigenous peoples of the Americas

The population figure for Indigenous peoples in Americas before the 1492 voyage of Christopher Columbus has proven difficult to establish. Scholars rely on archaeological data and written records from settlers from the Old World. Most scholars writing at the end of the 19th century estimated the pre-Columbian population at about 10 million, by the end of the 20th century the scholarly consensus had shifted to about 50 million, with some arguing for 100 million or more. Contact with the New World led to the European colonization of the Americas, in which millions of immigrants from the Old World eventually settled in the New World.

The population of African and Eurasian peoples in the Americas grew steadily, while the number of the indigenous people plummeted. Eurasian diseases such as smallpox, influenza, bubonic plague and pneumonic plagues devastated the Native Americans who did not have immunity. Conflict and outright warfare with Western European newcomers and other American tribes further reduced populations and disrupted traditional society. The extent and causes of the decline has long been a subject of academic debate, along with its characterization as a genocide

List of epidemics that Mr. God, send to the   earth, most people believe is a loving father, Mr. God I will give you a list of most diseases that you know, include the death toll.

Europe (1346-1350) known as "Black Death" or "Black Plague" kill Toussaint

Mexico (1576) Cocolitztli viral hemorrhagic fever

Seneca nation 1576-1596, Measles

Spain 1596-1602 plague

South America 1600-1650

England 1603 London plague

Egypt 1609 plague

Southern New England, especially the Wampanoag people 1616-1619 Unknown cause. Latest research suggests epidemic of leptospirosis with Weil syndrome. Classic explanations include yellow fever, bubonic plague, influenza, smallpox, chickenpox, typhus, and syndemic infection of hepatitis B and hepatitis D

Italy (1629-1631, death toll 280,000, Italian plague

Ontario Smallpox 1630

China 1641-1644 helped end the Ming Dynasty plague

Spain 1647-1652 Great Plague of Seville plague

South America 1648 yellow fever

Italy 1656 Naples plague

Netherlands 1663-1666 Amsterdam plague, death toll 24,148

England 1665-1666 Great Plague of London plague, death toll 100,000

France 1668, plague, death toll 40,000

Spain 1676-1685 plague

Austria 1679 Great Plague of Vienna plague

Sweden 1710-1711 Stockholm plague

Canada, New France 1714-1715 measles

France 1720-1722 Boston, Massachusetts measles

Canada, New France 1733 smallpox

Balkans 1738 Great Plague of 1738 plague

Italy 1743 Messina plague

North America 1755-1756 smallpox

North America, West Indies 1761 influenza

Russia 1770-1772 Russia plague

United States 1788 Philadelphia and New York measles

United States 1793 Vermont influenza and epidemic typhus

United States 1793-1798 Yellow Fever Epidemic of 1793, resurgences yellow fever

Ottoman Empire, Egypt 1801 bubonic plague

United States 1803 New York yellow fever

Egypt 1812 plague

Ottoman Empire 1812 Istambul plague

Malta 1813 plague

Romania 1813 Bucharest plague

Ireland 1816-1819 typhus

Iran 1829-1835 bubonic plague

Egypt 1831 cholera

England, France 1832 London, Paris cholera

North America 1832 New York City, Montreal other cities cholera

United States 1833 Columbus, Ohio cholera

United States 1834 New York cholera

Egypt 1834-1836 bubonic plague

United States 1837 Philadelphia typhus

Great Plains 1837-1838 1837—38 smallpox epidemic

Dalmatia 1840 plague

South Africa 1840 Cape Town smallpox

United States 1841 especially severe in the South yellow fever

20,000+ Canada 1847-1848 Typhus epidemic of 1847 epidemic typhus

United 1847 New Orleans yellow fever

Worldwide 1847-1848 influenza

Egypt 1848 cholera

North America 1848-01849 cholera

United States 1850 yellow fever

North America 1850-1851 influenza

United States 1851 Illinois, the Great Plains, and Missouri cholera

United States 1852- New Orleans yellow fever

1,000,000 Russia 1852-1860 Third cholera pandemic cholera

Ottoman Empire 1853, which now Yemen plagues

616 England 1854 Broad Street cholera outbreak cholera

United States 1855 yellow fever

Worldwide 1855-1950 Third Pandemic bubonic plague

Portugal 1857 Lisbon yellow fever

Victoria, Australia 1857 smallpox

Europe, North America, South America 1857-1859 influenza

Middle East 1863-1879 fourth cholera pandemic cholera

Egypt 1865 cholera

Russia, Germany 1866-1867 cholera

Australia 1867 Sydney measles

Iraq 1867 plague

Argentina 1852-1871 Buenos Aires yellow fever

Germany 1870-1871 smallpox

Fiji 1875 40,000 measles

Russian Empire 1877 Baku, now consider part of Azerbaijan plague

Egypt, 1881 cholera

>>9,000 India, Germany 1881-1896 fifth cholera pandemic cholera

3, 164 Montréal 1885 smallpox timeline

1,000,000 worldwide 1889-1890 flu pandemic influenza

Congo Basin 1896-1906 trypanosomiasis

>>800,000 Europe, Asia Africa 1899-1932 sixth cholera pandemic cholera

113 San Francisco 1900-1904 Third plague pandemic bubonic

West Africa 1900 yellow fever

Uganda 1900-1920 trypanosomiasis

Egypt 1903 cholera

India 1903 plague

China 1910-1912 Manchuria bubonic plague

75,000,000 worldwide 1918-1920, 1918 flu pandemic influenza

Russia 1918-1922 typhus

Egypt 1942-1944 malaria

China 1946 Manchuria bubonic plague

Egypt, 1946 relapsing fever

2,000,000 worldwide 1957-1958 Asian flu influenza

Worldwide 1961-present seventh cholera pandemic cholera

1,000,000 worldwide 1968-1969 Hong Kong flu influenza

(5) Netherlands 1971 Staphorst, Elspeet and Uddel Poliomyelitis

Yugoslavia 1972, outbreak of smallpox in Yugoslavia smallpox

United States 1972-1973 London flu influenza

15,000 India 1974 1974 smallpox epidemic of India smallpox

>>30,000,000 worldwide 1981-present HIV/AIDS pandemic HIV/AIDS

South America 1990s cholera

52 India 1994 1994 plagues in Surat Plague

West Africa 1996 meningitis

Central America 2000 dengue fever

Nigeria 2001 cholera

South Africa 2001 cholera

775 Asia 2002-2003 SARS SARS conronavirus

Algeria 2003 plague

Afghanistan 2004 leishmaniasis

Bangladesh 2004 cholera

Indonesia 2004 dengue fever

Senegal 2004 cholera

Sudan 2004 Ebola

Mail 2005 yellow fever

19 Singapore 2005, 2005 dengue outbreak in Singapore dengue fever

Angola 2006 Luanda cholera

Congo 2006 Ituri Province plague

India 2006 malaria

50+ India 2006 2006 dengue outbreaks in India (dengue fever)

India 2006 Chikungunya outbreaks (Chikungunya virus)

50+ Pakistan 2006 2006 dengue outbreaks in Pakistan dengue fever

Philippines 2006 dengue fever

Congo 2007 Mweka ebola

Ethiopia 2007 cholera

49 India 2007 cholera

10 Iraq 2007 2007 Iraq cholera outbreak cholera

Nigeria 2007 Poliomyelitis

Puerto Rico, Dominican Republic, Mexico 2007 dengue fever

Somalia 2007 cholera

Uganda 2007 Ebola

Vietnam 2007 cholera

Brazil 2008 dengue fever

Cambodia 2008 dengue fever

Chad 2008 cholera

China 2008 hand, foot and mouth disease

Madagascar 2008 bubonic plague

Philippines 2008 dengue fever

Vietnam 2008 cholera

4,293 Zimbabwe 2008-2009 (2008, 2009 cholera outbreak)

18 Bolivia 2009, (dengue fever epidemic)

India 2009. 2009 Gujarat hepatitis B outbreak

Queensland, Australia 2009 dengue fever

Worldwide 2009 Mumps outbreaks in the 2000s mumps

931 West Africa 2009-2010 West Africa meningitis outbreaks

14,286 worldwide 2009-2010 (flu pandemic influenza)

6,500+ (January 2012) Hispaniola (2010- 2011 Haiti cholera outbreak)

Congo 2011 measles

81 Vietnam 2011 hand, foot and mouth disease

350+ Pakistan 2011 dengue fever outbreaks

89+ (April 2014) Guinea Ebola outbreak

 List of people who were beheaded by you name, but they didn't received any protection (mercy or grace) Gnaeus Pompeius (45BC), Pompey'son executed for treason by Julius Caesar

Titus Labienus (45BC)-general, politician and one of Julius Caesar's foremost subordinates, killed and beheaded posthumously at the battle of Munda

Gaius Trebonius (43BC), politician and general, toutured and be headed by Pubius Cornelius Dolabella, his head was kicked around like a football by Dolabella's soldiers

Cicero (43BC), politician, lawyer and Rome's greatest orator executed by order of Marc Anthony

Marcus Antonius Antyllus (30BC), son of Marc Antony, executed by Octavian.

Galba (69) - assassinated Roman emperor.

Pope Stephen I (257)-Christian Martyr executed by Emperor Valerian.

Pope Sixtus II (258)-Christian Martyr executed by Emperor Valerian.

Stilicho (408)-executed in coup d'état after Gothic invasion

Anthemius (472)-Emperor-Assassinated by Ricimer.

Medieval Italy:

Giordano d'Anglano (1267), beheaded in Brolo, Sicily by Charles of Anjou after the Battle of Tagliacozzo.

Conradin, King of Sicily (29 October 1268), executed in Naples by Charles of Anjou.

Frederick I of Baden, Margrave of Baden (29 October 1268), executed in Naples by Charles of Anjou.

Later Italy:

Marino Faliero, Doge of Venice(1355), executed for a failed coup d'état

Antongaleazzo Bentivoglio (1435), beheaded in Bologna as a rebel

Gian Paolo Baglioni (1520), beheaded in Rome for attempted assassination

Giovanni Carafa, Duke of Paliano (1561), beheaded by order of Pope Pius

Pietro Carnesecchi (1567, beheaded by the inquisition for heresy

Beatrice Cenci and Lucrezia Peroni (1599), beheaded by sword in Rome for murder of Francesco Cenci.

Ferrante Pallavicino (1644), beheaded at Avignon for blasphemy by order of Pope Urban VIII

Felice Orsini (1858), executed by Napoleon III for attempting to assassinate him.

Jochen Rindt (!970), Partially decapitated by lap belt of his lotus 72 in a crash during practice for the 1970 Italian Grand Prix at Monza. Even though his lotus didn't have any wings the crash wasn't caused by the lack of wings, the crash was caused by the input shaft to the front brakes failing and pitching the car into a fencepost smashing the nose and causing Rindt to slide out the through the shattered nose by centrifugal force of the spinning car, Rindt agreed to using a lap belt but not a crotch strap. If he did, he wouldn't have been killed in the accident.

The execution of Marino Faliero, Eugene Delacroix, 1827

Giovani Battista Bugatti, executioner of the Papal States, between 1796 and 1865, carried out 516 executions.

Japan:

Ishida Mitsunari, daimyo and general (1600) beheaded in Kyoto after the Battle of Sekigahara

Ankokuji Ekei, Buddhist monk and ally of Mitsunari (1600), beheaded in Kyoto after the Battle of Sekigahara.

Asano Naganori, lord of the forty-seven Ronin (1701), ordered to commit seppuku followed by beheading.

Kondo Isami, commander of the Shinsengumi (1868), executed at Itabashi.

Japanese occupied territories (20th century):

Leonard Siffleet (1943), Australian soldier executed in Papua New Guinea by Japanese captors.

Stanley James Woodbridge, British RAF crewman (1945) captured and beheaded by Japanese forces in Burma.

Kim Okgyun, Korean activist (1894) assassinated and beheaded at sea by hong Jong-u due to leading Gapsin Revolution.

Netherlands/Belgium

Wijerd Jelckama (1523) executed in Leeuwarden for the Frisian rebellion.

Jan van Casembroot (1568) beheaded by the governor, the Duke of Alba, at Vilvoorde for treason

Lamoral, Count of Egmont (1568) beheaded in Brussels for treason.

Philip de Montmorency, Count of Horn (1568) beheaded in Brussels for treason.

Johan van Oldenbarnevelt (1619) executed. The Hague for Holland separatism by Prince Maurice.

Chris Bristow (1960), Decapitated in racing car crash.

Ottoman Empire:

Thousands of Christian crusades (1396) executed by Ottoman Sultan Bayezid I after Battle of Nicopolis in retaliation of the executions of thousands of Muslim soldiers fighting to conquer Christian lands.

Ali Pasha (1822) shot and beheaded by order of Sultan Mahmud II.

Pakistan:

Northwest India before 1947, Raja Dahir (712) executed on command of Muhammad Bin Qasim after Dahir's empire was defeated.

Islamic Republic of Pakistan, Daniel Pearl (2002), American journalist killed by terrorists.

Austria:

Joseph Haydn (1809)-celebrated composer posthumously beheaded: see Haydn's head

Africa:

Tom Pryce (1977)-racing driver partially decapitated by chin strap

Canada:

Tim Mclean (2008)-murdered and decapitated on Greyhound bus

Roberta McIvor (2008)-found decapitated alongside dirt road

Fribjon Bjornson (2012)-severed head found on the Nak'azdli reserve near Fort St. James

Robert John Roth (2012)-served head found in Edmonton alley

China:

Guan Yu (219)- Executed during civil war by Sun Quan

Wen Tianxiang (1283) - scholar and general

Adolf Schlagintweit (1857) - German botanist and explore; executed by the ruler of Kashgar

Tan Sitong (1898) - Executed with five others by Empress Dowager Cixi

Chile:

Maria Jose Reyes and Juan Duarte (2012)- Beheaded by a seller of antiquities in Lolo

Denmark:

Anne Palles (1693) - Executed in Copenhagen for witchcraft

Johann Friedrich Struenssee (1772) - Executed in Copenhagen for lese-majeste

Enevold Brandt (1772) - Executed in Copenhagen for lese-Majeste

England:

Waltheof, Earl of Northumbria (1076)- Executed at Winchester by order of William 1 for taking part in the Revolt of the Earls

Sir William Wallace (1305)- famous Scottish resistance fighter, hanged, drawn and quartered by order of Edward 1

Piers Gaveston(1312)- Executed near Warwick by Thomas, 2nd Earl of Lancaster in the Baron's Revolt

Thomas, 2nd Earl of Lancaster- Lord High Steward (1322)-Executed at Pontefract by Edward III

Edmund FitzAlan, 9th Earl of Arundel (1326) - Executed at Hereford by Queen Isabella, Regent for Edward III

Edmund of Woodstock, 1st Earl of Kent- Lord Wardens of the Clique Ports (1330)- Executed at Winchester by Queen Isabella, Regent for Edward

Sir Robert Hales- Lord High Treasure (1381) - Executed at Tower Hill by rebels during the Peasants' Revolt

Simon of Sudbury- Lord Chancellor, Archbishop of Canterbury and Bishop of London (1381)- Executed at Tower Hill by rebels during the Peasants' Revolt

British North America:

Wingina (15860- Roanoke Indian chief executed by first English settlers in the New World

Metacomet (1676)- New England Indian chief "King Philip" executed for resisting white settlement

Panama:

Vasco Nunez de Balboa (1519)- Spanish conquistador who slipcovered the Pacific Ocean. Executed by rivals Francisco Pizarro and Pedro Arias de Avila

Haiti:

Dutty Boukman (1791)- Executed by the French for promoting a slave rebellion

Brazil:

Joaquim Jose da Silcva Xavier (tiradentesa0 (1792)- the body was quartered after his hanging for revolutionary activity

Mexico:

Miguel Hidalgo y Costilla and Lgnacio Allende (1811)- Mexican insurgents were beheaded after their execution by firing squad

Bolivia:

Manuel Ascencio Padilla (1816)- Executed for insurrection after the Battle of La Laguna

Peru:

Diego de Almagro (1548) - Executed in Peru by Pedro de la Gasca for rebellion

Finland:

Tahvo Purkonen (1825) - beheaded for murder. This was the last beheading in finland

France:

Olivier III de Clisson (1343) - Executed by Philip VI of France for treason

Jean de Montaigu (1409) - Executed in Paris by Charles VI of France

Gabriel de Lorges, Cmte de Montgomery (1574)- Executed by Catherine de Medici for treason

Henri de Talleyrand-pergord, comte de Chalais (1626)- Executed in Nates for conspiracy against Cardinal Richelieu

Jean-Francois de la Barre (1766) - Beheaded and burnt in Abbeville for blasphemy

Restoration:

Four Sergeants of La Rochelle (1822) - Executed for treason against Louis XVIII of France

Giuseppe Marco Fieschi (1836) - Executed by guillotine for attempting to assassinate King Louis-Philippe

French Republic:

Francois Claudius Koenigstein, known as Ravachol (1892) - Guilotined for murder and anarchy

Sante Geronimo Caserio (1894) - Executed for assassination of President Marie Francois
Sadi Carnot

Teophile Derco, the "pollet Band" (1909)- guillotined in Behune (Nord-Pas-de-Calais), by Anatole Deibler, for a series of murders

Canut Vromant, the "Pollet Band" (1909)- guillotined in Bethune (Nord-Pas-de-Calais), by Anatole Deibler, for a series of murders

Auguste Pollet, the "Pollet Band" (1909)- guillotined in Behune (Nord-Pas-de-Calais), Anatole Deibler, for a series of murders

Abel Pollet, the "Pollet Band" (1909)-guillotined in Bedthune (Nord-Pas-de-Calais), by Anatole Deibler, for a series of murders

Henri Landur (1922) - Executed for serial murder

Paul Gorguloff (1922)-Executed in Paris for assassination of President Paul Doumer

Eugen Weidmann (1939) - Executed for murder. Last public execution by guillotine in France

Jean Lariviere (1951) - decapitated in racing car crash

Some spectator of the 1955 Le Mans disaster

Jaques Fesch (1957) - Executed in Paris for killing a policeman

Christian Rancucci (1976)-guillotined in Douai for murder

Jerome Carrein (1977)-guilotined in Marseille formurder

Hamida Djandoubi (1977) - guillotined in Marseille for murder- last guillotine execution

Georgia:

Demtre II (1289) - Executed by the Mongol Arghun Khan for rebellion

Germany:

Priscillian (385) - Beheaded for heresy at Trier

Klaus Stortebeker (1400) - Beheaded for being a pirate in Hamburg

Thomas Muntzer (1525) - Beheaded after the Battle of Frankenhausen during German Peasants' War

Ludwig Hactzer (1529) - Executed in Konstanz for Protestant radicalism (but technically for adultery)

Schinderhannes (1803) - Guillotined in Mainz for armed robbery and other crimes

Max Hodel (1878) - Executed for attempting to assassinate Emperor Wilhelm I

Welmar Republic:

Fritz Haarmann (1925) - The Butcher (or Vampire) of Hanover- Guillotined in Hanover for murder

Peter Kurten (1931)- the Vampire of Susseldorf- Gullotined in Colugne for murder

Nazi Germany:

Bruno Tesch (1933) - Executed in Altona with three other after "Altona Bloody Sunday"

Mainus van der Lubbe (1934)- Gullotined in Lipzig for starting the Reichstag fire

Benita von Falkenhayn and Renate Von Natzmer (1935) - Executed by axe in Berin for espionage

Edgar Josef Andre' (1936) - Beheaded in Hamburg for treasonous involvement in the Reichstag fire

Helmut Hirsch (1937) - Executed in Berlin for treason

Lilo Hermann (1938) - Guillotined in Berlin for "Attempting to assassinate Hitler

Helmuth Hubener (1942) - Guillotined in Berlin for treason

LLse Sstobe (1942) - Guillotined in Berlin for treason via Red Orchestra

Franz Jagerstatter(1943)- Guillotined in Berlin as a conscientious objector

Maria Restituta (1943) - Guillotined for treason

Cato Bontjes van Beck (1943) - Guillotined in Berlin for conspiracy to commit treason

Julius Fuckfk (1943) - Guillotined in Berlin for anti-Nazi activity via Whitee Rose resistance group

Christoph Pobst (1943) - Guillotined for treson via White Rose resistance group

Willi Grag (1943) - Guillotined for treason via White Rose resistance group

Otto and Elise Hampel (1943) - Guillotined in Berlin for treason

Musa Calil (1944) - Guillotined in Berlin for anti-Nazi activities

Werner Seelenbinder (1944) - beheaded with an axe, for being a communist

Fredrich Lorenz (1944) - beheaded by Nazi party at Halle ea der Saale

Post-war Germany

Herbert Muller (1981)- decapitated in racing car

Great Britain:

Willian Gordon, 6th Viscount of Knmure (1716)- executed at Tower Hill as a Jacobite Rebel

James Radclyffe, 3rd Earl of Derwentwater (1716)- executed at Tower Hill as a Jacobite Rebel

Arthur Elphinstone, 6th Lord Balmerinoch (1746)- beheaded at Tower Hill as a Jacobite suppoeter of Prince Charles Edward Stuart, he was taken prisoner at Culloden

William Boyd, 4th Earl of Kilmarnock (1746)- beheaded at Tower Hill as a Jacobite supporter of Prince Charles Edward Stuart, he was taken prisoner at Culloden

Charles Radclyffe, titular 5th Earl of Derwentwater (1746)- executed at Tower Hill as Jacobite Rebel

Simon Fraser, 11th Lord Lovat (1747)- executed at Tower Hill as a prominent veteran Jacobite supporter of Prince Charles Edward Stuart. Though too old to participate in the 1745 Rising, he was chose by the British Crown for Execution in lieu o his youthful son, who has actually led Clan Fraser for the Jacobite cause

Jermiah Brandreth (1817)- hanged and beheaded in Derby for treson; last Brtitish decapitation by axe

Hon. Henry William John, later 4th Earl of Starfford (1899)- decapitated by a train

Jolanta Bledaite (2008)- Lidhuanian immigrant, totured and killed in Scotland

Gerald Mellin (2008)- list of unusual deaths

David Phyall (2008)- list of unusual deaths

Hungary:

Laszlo Hunyadi (1457)- Exevuted by Ladislaus V for plot6ting aginst him

India:

Guru Tegh Bahadur (1675)- Ninth guru of Sikhs excuted in Delhi by order of Mogul empero Aurangezeb

Raja Dahir (712) - ecevuted on command of Muhammad bin Qasim after Dahir's Kingdom of Sindh was defeated

Iraq:

Shosei Koda (2004)- Japanese citizen beheaded by terrorists

Kim Sun-il (2004)- UK citizen beheaded by terroists

Nick Berg (2004)- US citizen beheaded by terrorists

Eugene Armstrong (2004) - US citizen beheaded by terrorists

Jack Hensley (2004) - US citizen beheaded by terrorists

Paul Marshall Johson, Jr. (2004) - US citizen beheaded by terrorists

Barzan Ibrahim al-Tikriti (2007)- Saddam Hussein's half-brother decapitated during hanging for crimes against humanity

Ireland:

Lucius Appuleius Saturninus (100BC0- radical tribune; Gaius Rabirius toyed with his severed head at a dinner party

Marcus Antonius Orartor (87BC)- grandfather of Marc Antony

Marcus Marius Gratidianus (82 BC0, praetor5 whose head was paraded through Rome after execution

Gaisu Marcius Censorinus (general) (82 BC), beheaded by Sulla, his head was sent to Preneste to lower Gaius Marius the Younger's troop's morale

Marcus Licintus Crassus (53 BC)- general, politician and richest man then in the world- beheaded posthumously after his defeat in Parthia

Publius Licinius Crassus (53 BC)- son of Marcus Licinius Crassus – beheaded posthumously in Parhia

Pompey the Great (48 BC)- general, politician and member of the First Trimvirate- assassinated and beheaded posthumously in Egypt

Poland:

Kazimierz alyszczynski (1689) - executed in Warsaw for heresy

Russia:

Stenka Razin (1671) - Quartered alive in Moscow for Cossack revolution

Mary Hamilton (lady in waiting) (1719) - executed for infanticide and slandering Catherine I of Russia

Yeemelyan Pugachev (1775) - Executed in Moscow for insurrection by Catherine II of Russia

Yevgeny Rodionov (1996) - Beheaded by Chechen terrorists

Saudi Arabia:

Prince Faisal bin Musa'id (1975) - for the assassination of his uncle, the king

Paul Marshall Johnson, Jr. (2013) - Sri Lankan wowan for homicide

Scotland:

Donnchadh, Earl of Lennox (1425) - Executed by orders of James I of Scotland

Lord Walter Stewart and Lord Alexander Sewart (1425) - Executed by order of Jame Scotland

Murdoch Stewart, Duke of Albany (1425) - Executed by order of James I of Scotland

Walter Stewart, 1st Earl of Douglas (14370- Executed for his part in the murder of James I of Scotland

William Douglas, 6th Earl of Douglas (1440) - Executed on trumped-up charges in front of James II of Scotland

Hugh Douglas, Lord of Balvenie (1463) - Executed on the orders of James III of Scotland

John Douglas, Lord of Balcenie (1463) - Executed on the orders of James III of Scotland

Sir James Hamiltion of Finnart- Master of Work to the Crown of Scotland (1540)- Executed by order of James V of Scotland

James Douglas, 4th Earl of Morton (1581) - Executed on the Scottish maiden for complicity in murder of Lord Darnley

William Ruthven, 1st Earl of Gowrie (1584) - Executed by order of James VI of Scotland

John Maxwell, 9th Lord Maxwell (1613) - Beheaded in Edinburgh for carrying out a revenge killing

Parick Sstewar, 2nd Earl of Orkney (1615) - Executed by order o James VI of Scotland

Sir John Gordon, 1st Baronet of Haddo (1644)- Executed on the Scottish maiden by the Covenanters for treason as a Royalist

Archibald Campbell, 1st Marquess of Argyll (1661)- Executed by order of Charles II of Scotland on the Scottish maiden for treason

Archibald Campbell, 9th Earl of Argyll (1685)- son of above. Executed by order of James VII of Scotland on the Scottish maiden for treason

Godfrey Mcculloch (1697) - Executed on the Scottish maiden for murder. Last man to be executed

Spain:

Eulogius of Cordova (1859) - Executed by Muslim rulers for blasphemy

Rodrigo Calderon (1621) - Executed in Madrid

Antonio Osorio de Acuna (1526) - Executed in Simancas for supportin the Comunero Revolt

Juan Bravo (1521)- Executed in Villalar de los Comuneros, Valladolid

Juan de Padilla (1521) - Executed in Villalar de los comuneros, Valladolid

Francisco Maldonado (1521) - Executed in Villalar de Los Comuneros, Valladolid

Sri Lanka:

Keppetiola Disawe (1818) - Executed in Kandy, Sri Lanka

Sweden:

Mattias Gregersson (1520) - Bishop of Strangnas. Executed by Danes in the Stockholm Bloodbath

Vincent Henningsson (1520) - Bishop of Skara. Executed by Danes in the Stockholm Bloodbath

Anna Zippel (1676) - Executed in Stockholm for witchcraft

Brita Zippel (1676) - sister of above. Executed in Stockholm for witchcraft

Gavle Boy (1676) - witness in the trial against the above sisters. Executed for perjury

Anna Eriksdotter (1704) - beheaded for sorcery.

Jacob Johan Anckarstrom (1792) - executed for assassination of Gustv III

Metta Fock (1810) - executed for murder of her husband and children.

Anna Mansotter (1890) Executed by axe for murder. Last woman executed in Sweden

John fillip Nordlund (1900) - Executed by axe in Vasteras for mass murder

Johan Alfred Ander (1910) Executed by guillotine in Stockholm for murder. Last Swedish execution

Switzerland:

Wildhans von Breitenlandenberg and 61 companions following the siege of Greifensee during the Old Zurich War (1444)

Anna Goldi (1782) - Executed as the last witch in Switzerland

United States:

Isaac N. Ebey (1857) - Washington state pioneer murdered by Haida Indians

Pearl Bryan (1896) - Murdered in Fort Thomas, Kentucky

Tom Kechum (1901) - accidentally decapitated in New Mexico Territory in botched handing for train robbery

Charles Bassett (1966) - decapitated in crash of jet aircraft

Francois Cevert (1974) - decapitated in crash of jet aircraft

Helmuth Koinigg (1974) - decapitated in racing car crash

16 victim of Jeffery Dahmer (1978- 1991)

Boris Sagal (1981) - partially decapitated by helicopter

Adam Walsh (1981) - decapitated by murderer

Gordon Smiley 919820- partially decapitated in racing car crash

Vic Morrow and Myca Dinh Le (1982)- decapitated by crashing helicopter during film shoot

Christa Hoyt (1990) - decapitated by serial killer Danny Rolling

Nicole Brown Simpson (1994) - partially decapitated by murderer

Russell Phillips (1995)- decapitated in racing car crash

Robert Lees (2004)- decapitated by murderer

Asisya Zubair (20090- decapitated in New York State by murederer/husband

Vietnam:

Vicente Liem de la Paz (1773) - Beheaded in Tonkin as Christian martyr

Pierre Dumoulin-Borie (1838) - Beheaded in Tonkin as Christian martyr

Bernard Vo Van Due (1838) - Beheaded in Korea as Christian martyr

Andrew Dung-Lac (1839) - Beheaded in Korea as Christian martyr

Augustin Schoeffler (1851) - Beheaded in Tonkin as Christian martyr

Jean- Louis Bonnard (1852) - Beheaded in korea as Christian martyr

Theophane Venard (1861) - Beheaded in Tonkin as Christian martyr

Ba Cut (Le Quang Vinh) (1956) - Guillotined in Can Tho for insurrection and multiple murder

Wales:

Gwenllian Ferch Gruffudd (February 1136) - executed by the Anglo- Norman forces led by Maurice de Londres at Kidwelly Castle, Walse, after a failed uprising

Llewelyne ap Gruffydd (1282) - Beheaded posthumously after his death in battle at Aberedw.

Sir Gruffudd Vychan (1447) - Executed at Powis Castle by Lord Powis for unclear reasons.

Sir Roger Vaughan (1471) - Beheaded at Chepstow by Jasper Tudor, Earl of Bedford for being a Yorkist.

Catholic saints:

Saint Acisclus

Saint Agnes

Saint Alban (around 304)- Executed in Britain by Romans for Converting to Christianity

Saint Ansanus

Saint Anthumus of Rome

Saint Catherine of Alexandria

Saint Christopher

Saint Columba of Spain (c853) - Executed in Spain by Moors for not converting to Islam

Saint Columba of France

Saint Columba (the Virgin) of Cornwall, England

Saints Columba and Damian (c.287) - Executed by Emperor Diocletian in purge of Christians in Syria

Saint Cyprina (258)- Bishop of Carthage, North Africa- Christian Martyr executed by Emperor Valerian

Saint Denis, who carried his head to his final resting place, a familiar hagiographical trope

Saint Diomeded

Saint Dymphna

Saint Emmeram

Saint Euroisa

Saint Felicitas of Rome

Saint Felix and Nabor

Saints Firmus and Rusticus

St Francis de Capillas (1648)- Beheaded at Forgan, China

Saint George

Saint Gereon

Saint Gordianus

Saint James, traditionally

Saint John Fisher (1535) - beheaded in London for treson

Saint John de Brito (1693) - executed in India for preaching Christianity

Saint Marcellus

Saint Mazimilian (295) - Executed by Romans for conscientious objection to military services

Saint Nicasius of Rheims, at Rheims (407) - Executed by Vandals during conquest of Rheims

Saint Oliver Plunkett (1681)- Hung, drawn and quartered in London for treason

Saint Pancras

Apostle Paul, traditionally

Saint Quiteria

Saints Rufina and Secunda

Saints Simplicius and Faustinus

Saint Urith of Chittlehampton, Devon, England

Saint Venantius at Camerino

Mr. God when are you going to be able to stop Genocide? Rape, war, think yourself, how many people lost their life in Rwanda, you was there, what the reason you can protect this world, most of you religion leaders, campaigning that , you still waiting for judgment, and you are incapable to stop all atrocities. Mr. God, let me explain about Rwanda genocide in Africa.

Methods of force and threat, the genocidairess forced others to stand by while women were raped. A testimonial by a woman of the name Maria Louise recalls seeing local peoples, other generals and Hutu men watching her get raped about five times per day. Even when she was kept under watch of a woman, she would give no sympathy or help and furthermore, forced her to farm land in between rapes

Many of the survivors were also infected with the HIV virus transmitted from from the HIV-infected men who were recruited by the genocidaires. During the conflict Hutu extremists released hundreds of patients from hospitals, who were suffering from AIDS, and formed them into "rape squads". The intent was to infect and cause a "Slow, inexorable death". Tutsi women were also targeted with the intent of destroying their reproductive capabilities. Sexual mutilation sometimes occurred after the rape and included mutilation of the vagina with machetes, knives, sharpened sticks, boiling water, and acid. Men were seldom the victims of war, rape. There was an attempt to eliminate Tutsis and erase any memory of their existence. Carried out by Nazi Germany and the Khmer Rouge in Cambodia, authorities made no attempts to record deaths. The succeeding RPF government has stated that 1,071,000 were killed, 10% of whom were Hutu. The journalist Phillip Gourevitch agrees with an estimates of one million, while the UN estimates the toll as 800,000. Alex de Waal and Rakiya Omar of African Rights estimate the number as "around 750,000" While Alison Des Forges of Human Rights Watch states that it was at least 500.000

What's important to remember is that there was genocide.

Out of a population of 7.3 million people-84% of whom were Hutu, 15% Tutsi, the officials figures published by the Rwandan government estimated the number of victims of the genocide to be 1,174,000", thousands of widows, many of whom were subjected to rape, are now HIV-positive. There were about 400,000 orphans and nearly 85,000 of them were forced to become heads of families.

In January 1994, Dallaire was put in contact with a top-level trainer of the MDRP's interhamwe militia by a very important government politician. As a result of this conversation, Dallaire was able to send a fax to the UN headquarters in New York detailing the planned anti-Tutsi genocide. The fax furnished the UN with such details as locations and the means to be used. Principal aim of Interhamwe in the past was to protect Kigali from RPF. Since UNAMIR mandate he has been ordered to register all Tutsi in Kigali. He suspects it is for their extermination. Example he gave was that in 20 minutes his personnel could kill up to 1000 Tutsis, the fax ends with Dallaire's recommendation that his informant be granted protection and evacuated out of Rwanda and the UN commander's expressed intention to verify the information. For whatever reason, perhaps bureaucracy, the early warning never spread far enough to enlist help from the Security Council

In addition, the UN peacekeepers were sent with specific instruction not to interfere unless a fellow peacekeeper or self was in danger. Under the United Nation's Capstone Doctrine peacekeepers were to exercise their own judgment in stopping the violence, however, it was the Job of the United Nations Security Council to use force.

The UN and its member states did not respond to the realities on the ground. In the midst of the escalating crisis for Tutsis, they directed L.t General Romeo Dallaire to focus UNAMIR on evacuating foreign nationals from Rwanda. Due to the change in orders, Belgian UN peacekeepers abandoned the Don Bosco Technical School, filled with 2,000 refugees. Hutu militants waited outside, drinking beer and chanting "Hutu Power "After the Belgians left, the militants entered and massacred everyone inside, including hundreds of children.

Four days later the Security Council voted to reduce UNAMIR to 270 men, by Resolution 912. Following the withdrawal of the Belgian forces. Dallaire consolidated his contingent of Canadian, Ghanaian, and Dutch soldiers in urban areas and tried to provide areas of safe control, his actions saved the lives of 32,000 people of different races. The administrative head of UNAMIR, former Cameroonian foreign minister Jacques-Roger Booh-Booh, has been criticized for downplaying the significance of Dallaire's reports and for holding close ties to the Hutu militant elite.

The US was reluctant to get involved in the local conflict in Rwanda and refused to label the killings as genocide, then –President Bill Clinton later publicly regretted that decision in a frontline television interview. Five years later, Clinton stated that he believed that if he had sent 5,000 U.S peacekeepers, more than 500,000 lives could have been saved.

The new Rwandan government, led by interim President Theodore Sindikubwabo, an ethnic Hutu, worked to minimize international criticism. Twanda at that time had a seat on the Security Council. Its ambassador argued that the claims of genocide in the country were exaggerated and that the government was doing all that it could to stop it.

The UN conceded that acts of genocide may have been committed on May 17, 1994. By that time, the Red Cross estimated that 500,000 Rwandans had been killed. The UN agreed to send 5,500 troops, mostly from African countries, to Rwanda. This was the original number of troops requested by General Dallaire before the killing escalated. The UN also requested 50 armored personnel carriers from the United States, the US army charged 6.5 million (USD) for transport alone. Deployment was delayed due to arguments over their cost and other factors.

Some UN peacekeepers protected Rwandans despite the organization limitations. One Senegalese peacekeeper, Mbaye Diagne, drove 1,000 people through check points to safety, a feat that no nation even attempted. Others stood outside of churches where hundreds of Tutsis refugees hid, their mere presence was sometimes enough to stop the militants.

Paul Rusesabagina, who saved over 1,000 people by sheltering them at the Hotel des Mille Collines, has said: In a sense things got better after the peacekeepers left. People realized no one was going to help them.

Former president Francois Mitterand considered the RPF invasion in October 1990 to constitute clear aggression by an Anglophone neighbor on a Francophone country. French government documents describe the RPF as part of an "Anglophone plot, involving the President of Uganda, to create an English-speaking "Tutsi-Land" and increase Anglophone influence at the expense of French influence. The policy of France was to avoid a military victory by the RPF. As a matter for the French presidency, this foreign policy was not referred to parliament.

Most of Rwanda's arms deals were negotiated through the Rwandan embassy in Paris. Other forms of military assistance the government of France gave the Rwandan government, prior to the genocide, including the provision of military advisers and technical assistants. Although no such official mandate was decreed by the French National to Belgian intelligence in Rwanda. French diplomats advised opposition politicians that if they wanted to stop the RPF, they had to give their support to President Habyarimana.

On June 22, with no sign of a UN deployment taking place, the Security Council authorized French forces to land in Goma, Zaire on a humanitarian mission. They deployed throughout southwest Rwanda in an area they called "Zone Turquoise" quelling the genocide and stopping the fighting there, but often arriving in areas only after genocidaires had expelled or killed Tutsi citizens. Again, controversy subsequently arose about French intent. According to HRW, Operation Turquoise had another purpose preventing a victory by the RPF. HRW reported that some military officers in Paris had talked openly of breaking the back of the RPF. It remains that there were no documented large-scale killings in Zone Turquoise once it was established. Thus, regardless of any other aims attributed to it, the French intervention helped to stop the genocide locally and represents the only foreign intervention on the ground to have ended some of the killings after UNAMIR was reduced. The French military presence effectively helped the genocidaires to escape from the RPF and flee into neighboring Zaire.

The suspicious about United Nations and French policies in Rwanda between 1990 and 1994 and allegations that France supported the Hutus led to the creation of a French Parliamentary Commission on Rwanda, which published its report on December 15,1998. In particular, Francois-Xavier Verschave, former president of the French NGO Survive, which accused the French army of protecting the Hutus during the genocide, was instrumental in establishing this Parliamentary commission. The commission released its final report on December 15, 1998. The report did not find any evidence of French participation in the genocide, of collaboration with the militias, or of willful disengagement from endangered populations. To the contrary, it documented multiple French operations, all at least partly successful, to disable genocide-inciting radio broadcasts, tasks which the UN and the United States had rejected calls for assistance with. The report concluded that there had been errors of Judgment pertaining to the broadcasts, tasks which the UN and the United States had rejected calls for assistance with. The report concluded that there had been errors of judgment pertaining to the genocide. Before the genocide, errors of Judgment about the scale of the threat, at the onset of the genocide, over-reliance on the UNAMIR mission without awareness that it would be undercut by the United States and other parties, and ineffective diplomacy. Ultimately, it concluded that France had been the foreign powers most involved in limiting the scale of the genocide once it started, though it regretted that more had not been done.

Between 9 April and 12 April French and Belgian aircraft and troops passed through the airport, evacuating almost all foreign nationals from the country. These troops were present solely to effect the evacuation, refusing to intervene to halt the ongoing killings or to admit any Rwandan refugees on the evacuations. After the RPF ended the genocide, in which three French crew also died, the French Judge Jean Louis Bruguiere indicted eight associates of Rwanda president Paul Kagame on November 17,2006, President Kagame himself was not indicted, as he had immunity under French law as a head of State. Kagame denied the allegations, decrying them as politically motivated, and broke diplomatic relationships with France in November 2006. He then ordered the formation of a commission of his own Rwandan Justice Ministry's employees that was officially" Charged with assembling proof of the involvement of France in the genocide. In July 2008, Kagame threatened to indict French nationals over the genocide if European courts did not withdraw arrest warrants issued against Rwandan officials, which by then included broader indictments against 40 Rwandan army officers by Spanish Judge Fernando Andreu. The Rwandan government shut down all French institutions in Rwanda, including schools and cultural organizations, with only some being subsequently reopened. The language of instruction in Rwandan school was switched from French to English, and Rwanda became one of only two members of the British-led Commonwealth that had not formerly been British colonies.

Findings of the commission were released at Kagame's order on August 5, 2008. The report accused the French government of knowing of preparations for the genocide and helping to train the ethnic Hutu militia members; it accused 33 senior French military and political officials of involvement in the genocide, including then-President Mitter and his then-general secretary Vedrine, then-Prime Minister Edouard Balladur, then-Forein Minister Alain Juppe, and his chief aide at the time, Dominique de Villepin. In 2010, during a visit to Rwanda, French President Nicolas Sarkozy acknowledged that France made mistakes during the genocide, although, according to BBC report, he stopped short of offering a full apology.　　`

Prior to the war, the U.S. government had aligned itself with Tutsi interests, in turn raising Hutu concerns about potential U.S. support to the opposition. Paul Kagame, a Tutsi officer in exile in Uganda who had co-founded the Rwandaise Patrioctic Front (RPF) in 1986 and was in open conflict with the incumbent Rwandan government, was invited to receive military training at Fort Leavenworth, Kansas, home of the Command and General Staff College, in 1990, while Kagame was at Fort Leavenworth, the RPF started an invasion of Rwanda. Only two days into the invasion, his close friend and RPF co-founder Fred Rwigyema was killed, upon which the U.S. arranged the return of Kagame to Uganda from where he became the military commander of the RPF. An article in the Washington Post of August 16,1997, written by its Southern African bureau chief Lynne Duke, indicates that the connection continued as RPF elements received counterinsurgency and combat training from U.S. Special Forces.

Intelligence reports indicate that President Clinton and his cabinet were aware before the height of the massacre that a final solution to eliminate all Tutsis was planned. Fear of a repeat of the events in Somalia shaped US policy in subsequent years, with many commentators identifying the graphic consequences of the Battle of Mogadishu as the key reason behind the US's failure to intervene in later conflicts such as the Rwandan Genocide of 1994. After the battle, the bodies of several US casualties of the conflict were dragged through the streets of Mogadishu by crowds of local civilians and Aidid's Somali National Alliance. According to the US's former deputy special envoy to Somalia, Walter Clarke: The ghosts of Somalia continue to haunt US policy. Our lack of response in Rwanda was a fear getting involved in something like a Somalia all over again. President Clinton has referred to the failure of the U.S. government to intervene in the genocide as one of his main foreign policy failing, saying "I don't think we could have ended the violence, but I think we could have cut it down. And I regret it.

Here in this message Clinton regret, but you Mr. God what was your reaction in this particular case, Genocide doesn't means nothing to you?

What was the reaction of the Vatican?

The Roman Catholic Church affirms that genocide took place but states that those who took part in it did so without the permission of the Church. Though religious factors were not prominent(the event was ethnically motivated) in its 1999 report Human Rights Watch faulted a number of religious authorities in Rwanda, including Roman Catholic, Anglican, and other Protestants for failing to condemn the genocide directly- though that accusation was belied over time. Some in its religious hierarchy have been brought to trial for their participation by the International Criminal for Rwanda and convicted. Bishop Misago was accused of corruption and complicity in the genocide, but he was cleared of all charges in 2000. Many other Catholic and Protestant clergy, however, gave their lives to protect Tutsis from slaughter. Some members of the clergy participated in the massacres. In 2006, Father Athanase Seromba was sentenced to 15 years imprisonment by the International Criminal Tribunal for Rwanda for his role in the massacre of 2000 Tutsis. The court heard that Seromba lured the Tutsis to the church, where they believed they would find refuge. When they arrived, he ordered bulldozers to crush the refugees within and Hutu militias to kill any survivors.

Mr. God? Do you remember what happen in Rwanda? Do you known what genocide means? The basis to be a world leader, God, super power God, God of God, the only God, this genocide is a part of you complicity, failing to condemn, failing to prevent, Mr. God I lost all my respect to you, the world need a better God, you're not a good God, you deserve a death sentence, no merci for you

The world had been put thousand people to death, most of them innocent, the only person who may have save them was you Mr. God, but you never show up to defend innocents people's, I have a list of people that the world put to the death without committed a crimes.

Capital punishment or the death penalty is a legal process whereby a person is put to death by the state as a punishment for a crime. The judicial decree that someone be punished in this manner is a death sentence, while the actual enforcement is an execution. Crimes that can result in a death penalty are known as capital crimes or capital offenses. The term capital originates from the latin capitalis, literally regarding the head (referring to execution by beheading)

Capital punishment has, in the past, been practiced by most societies, as a punishment for criminals, and political or religious dissidents. Historically, the carrying out of the death sentence was often accompanied by torture, and executions were most often public.

Currently 58 nations actively practice capital punishment, 98 countries have abolished it, 7 have abolished it for ordinary crimes only (maintain it for special circumstances such as war crimes), and 35 have abolished it, about 90%of all executions in the world take place in Asia. The world know that Mr. God was the architect of Death, Mr. God know that his is the only in charge to decide the death of human, but in this Capital punishment he just close his eyes, knowing he is the only can save people lives. What the role of God in this planet? Who is able to save people lives? Mr. God!

Capital punishment is a matter of active controversy in various countries and states, and positions can vary within a single political ideology or cultural region. In the European Union member states, Article 2 of the Charter of Fundamental Rights of the European Union prohibits the use of capital punishment. The Council of Europe, which has 47 member states, also prohibits the use of the death penalty by its members.

The United Nations General Assembly has adopted, in 2007, 2008 and 2010, non-binding resolutions calling for global moratorium on executions, with a view to eventual abolition. Although many nations have abolished capital punishment, over 60% of the world's population live in countries where executions take place, such as the People's Republic of China, India, the United States of America and Indonesia, the four most populous countries in the world, which continue to apply the death penalty, Each of these four nations voted against the General Assembly resolutions, Mr. God what you reaction?

Mr. God to you knows about Wrongful execution in this planet? What do you think for that?

Wrongful execution is a miscarriage of justice occurring when an innocent person is put to death by capital punishment "the death penalty". Cases of wrongful execution are cited as an argument by opponents of capital punishment.

A number of people are claimed to have been innocent victims of the death penalty. Newly available DNA evidence has allowed the exoneration and release of more than 15 death row inmates in the United States, but DNA evidence is available in only a fraction of capital cases. Others have been released on the basis of weak cases against them, sometimes involving prosecutorial misconduct, resulting in acquittal at retrial, charges dropped, or innocence-based pardons. The Death Penalty Information Center (U.S) has published a list of 10 inmates "executed but possibly innocent. At least 39 executions are claimed to have been carried out in the U.S. in the face of evidence of innocence or serious doubt about guilty. In the UK, reviews prompted by the Criminal Cases Review Commission have resulted in one pardon and three exonerations for people executed between 1950 and 1953, with compensation being paid.

Mr. God we have to many complaint against you in this court, included fail to protect a person in danger here is the cases of people's that was victim, but you didn't do nothing to protect them:

Weiging an, was a young Chinese, 23 years old, (Chinese citizen) who was executed for the rape of Liu, a woman who had disappeared. The execution was carried out on 3May 1984 by the Intermediate People's court. In the next month, Tian Yuxiu was arrested and admitted that he had committed the rape, God you are all over the world, when you powerfully leadership may have contributed to solve the situation in this planet? Mr. God!

Ten Xingsham was a Chinese citizen who was executed for supposedly having raped, robbed and murdered Shi Xiarong, a woman who had disappeared. An old man found a dismembered body, and incompetent police forensics claimed to have matched the body to the photo of the missing Shi Xiaorong. The execution was carried out on 28 January 1989 by the Huaihua Intermediate People's court. In 1993, the previously missing woman returned to the village, saying she had been kidnapped to Shandong. The absolute innocence of the wrongfully executed Teng was not admitted until 2005.

Nie Shubin was a Chinese citizen (1974-1995) who was executed for the rape and murder of Kang Juhua a woman in her thirties. The execution was carried out on April 27, 1995 by the Shijiazhuang Intermediate People's court. In 2005, ten years after the execution, Wang Shujin admitted to the police that, in fact, he had committed the murder.

Qoysiletu (Mongolian Chinese, 1977-1996) was an Inner Mongolian who was executed for the rape and murder of a young girl on June 10, 1996. On December 5, 2006, ten years after the execution, Zhao Zhihong, admitting that in fact he had committed the crime.

Johnny Garrett of Texas was executed February, 1992, for allegedly raping and murdering a nun. In March, 2004, cold-case DNA testing identified Leoncio Rueda as the rapist and murder of another elderly victim killed four months prior. Immediately following the nun's murder, prosecutors and police were certain the two cases were committed by the same assailant. In both cases, black curly head hairs were found on the victims, linked to Rueda. Previously unidentified fingerprints in the nun's room were matched to Rueda. The flawed case is explored in a 2008 documentary entitled "The last Word".

Jesse Tafero was convicted of murder and executed via electric chair May, 1990, in the state of Florida for the murders of two Florida Highway Patrol officers. The conviction of co-defendant was overturned in 1992 after a recreation of the crime scene indicated a third person had committed the murders.

Carlos Deluna was executed in Texas in December 1989. Subsequent investigations cast strong doubt upon Deluna's guilt for the murder of which he had been convicted.

Thomas and Meeks Griffin were executed in 1915 for the murder of a man involved in an interracial affair two years previously but were pardoned 94 years after execution. It is though that they were arrested and charged because they were viewed as wealthy enough to hire competent legal counsel and get an acquittal.

Chipita Rodriguez was hanged in San Patricio County, Texas in 1863 for murdering a horse trader, and 122 years later, the Texas legislature passed a resolution exonerating her. Mr. God what's going on with you? No assistance of person in danger?

Kirk Bloodsworth was the first American to be freed from death row as a result of exoneration by DNA fingerprinting. Ray Krone is the 100th American to have been sentenced to death and then later exonerated.

In the UK, reviews prompted by the Criminal Cases Review Commission have resulted in one pardon and three exonerations for people that were executed between 1950 and 1953. Timothy Evans was granted a posthumous free pardon in 1966. Mahmood Hussein Mattan was convicted in 1952 and was the last person to be hanged in Cardiff, Wales, but had his conviction quashed in 1998. George Kelly was hanged at Liverpool in 1998 with the appeal trial judge, Lord Bingham, nothing that the original trial judge, Lord Goddard, had denied the defendant "fair trial which is the birthright of every British citizen".

Colin Campbell Ross (1892-1922) was an Australian wine-bar owner executed for murder of a child which became known as The Gun Alley Murder, despite there being evidence that he was innocent. Following his execution, efforts were made to clear his name, and in 1990s old evidence was re-examined with modern forensic techniques which supported the view that Ross was innocent. In 2006 an appeal for mercy was made to Victoria's Chief Justice and on 27 May 2008, the Victorian government pardoned Ross in what is believed to be an Australian legal first. God you supposed to be involved in this particular assistance, because you the only know or shall have known what happen in this circumstance, but you can assist Justice to resolve this matter? Innocent people been hanged, knowing they didn't committed the crimes? When? Where? You presence in this world means something?

There has been much debate about the justification of imposing capital punishment on individuals who have been diagnosed with mental retardation. Some have argued that the execution of people with retardation constitutes cruel and unusual punishment as it pertains to the Eighth Amendment to the United States Constitution. And while the U.S. Supreme Court has interpreted cruel and unusual punishment to include those that fail into account the defendant's degree of criminal capability, it has not determined that executing the mentally retarded constitutes cruel and unusual punishment.

This issue was addressed in the case of "Penry v. Lynaugh, in which Johnny Paul Penry had filed a habeas corpus petition in federal district court that claimed his death sentence, should be vacated because it violated his Eight Amendment rights. His reasoning was that he suffered from mental retardation, and numerous psychologists had confirmed this to be factual, indicating that his IQ ranged from 50 to 63 and that he possessed the mental abilities of a six and a half-year-old. Penry's petition was denied by the district court, whose decision was subsequently affirmed by the Fifth Circuit Court of Appeals. Penry would later appeal to the U.S. Supreme Court, who ultimately ruled in a five-to-four decision that the Eight Amendment to the United States Constitution did not categorically prohibit the execution of persons with mental retardation. Following the 1989 Penry ruling, sixteen states as well as the federal government passed legislation that banned the execution of offenders with mental retardation.

Republic of China (Taiwan): Jiang Guoqing (1975-1997) was a Taiwanese soldier who was executed by a military tribunal on August 13, 1997 for the rape and murder of a five-year –old girl. On January 28, 2011, over 13 years after the execution, "Xu Rongzhou (Chinese citizen) admitted to the prosecutor that he had been responsible for the crime.

In 1660, in a series of events known as the Camden Wonder, an Englishman named William Harrison disappeared after going on a walk, near the village of Charingworth, in Glouccestershire. Some of his clothing was found slashed and bloody on the side of a local road. Police interrogated Harrison's servant, John Perry, who eventually confessed that his mother and his brother had killed Harrison for money. Perry, his mother, and his brother were hanged. Two years later, Harrison reappeared, telling the incredibly unlikely tale that he had been abducted by three horsemen and sold into slavery in Ottoman Empire. Though his tale was implausible, he indubitably had not been murdered by the Perry family.

Timothy Evans was tried and executed in 1950 for the murder of his baby daughter Geraldine. An official inquiry conducted 16 years later determined that it was Evans's fellow tenant, serial killer John Reginald Christie, who was responsible for the murder. Christie also admitted to the murder of Evans 'wife, as well as five other women and his own wife. Christie may have murdered other women, judging by evidence found in his possession at the time of his arrest, but it was never pursued by the police. Evans was posthumously pardoned in 1966. The case had prompted the abolition of capital punishment in the UK in 1965.

Mahmood Hussein Mattan was executed in 1952 for the murder of Lily Volpert. In 1998 the Court of Appeal decided that the original case was, in the words of Lord Justice Rose, "demonstrably flawed".

The families were awarded British money 725,000 compensation, to be shared equally among Mattan's wife and three children. The compensation was the first award for a person wrongfully hanged.

Mr. God, Republic of justice will never accept all you misconduct, negligence, failure to protect persons in danger, failure to prevent atrocities in this planet, what you reaction in this matter? Most religious leaders never denounce, you ineffectiveness leaderships in the earth.

Derek Bentley was a mentally challenged young man who was executed in 1953. He was convicted of the murder of a police officer during an attempted robbery, despite the facts that it was his accomplice who fired the gun and that Bentley was already under arrest at the time of the shooting. The accomplice who actually fired fatal shot could not be executed due to his young age.

United States: University of Michigan law professor, Samuel Gross led a team of experts in the law and in statistics that estimated the likely number unjust convictions. The study determined that at least 4%of people on death row were and is innocent. The research was peer reviewed and the prestigious Proceedings of the National Academy of Sciences published it, Gross has no doubt some innocent people have been executed.

Cameron Told Willingham was executed February, 2004, for murdering his three young children by arson at the family home in Corsicana, Texas. Nationally known fire investigator Gerald Hurst reviewed the case documents, including the trial transcriptions and an hour-long videotape of the aftermath of the fire and said in December 2004 that" There's nothing to suggest to any reasonable arson investigator that this was an arson fire. It was a fire. In 2010, the Innocence Project filed a lawsuit against the State of Texas, seeking a judgment of official oppression.

Statistics likely understate the actual problem of wrongful convictions because once an execution has occurred there is often insufficient motivation and finance to keep a case open, and it happen unlikely at that point that the miscarriage of justice will ever be exposed. In the case of Joseph Roger O'Dell III, executed in Virginia in 1997 for a rape and murder, a prosecuting attorney argued in court in 1998 that if posthumous DNA results exonerated O'Dell, it would be shouted the rooftops that.. Virginia executed an innocent man. The state prevailed, and the evidence was destroyed.

Opponents of the death penalty argue that this punishment is being used more often against perpetrators from racial and ethnic minorities and from lower socioeconomic backgrounds, than against those criminals who come from a privileged background, and that the background of the victim also influences the outcome. Researchers have shown that white Americans are more likely to support the death penalty when told that it is mostly applied to African Americans.

The United Nations introduced a resolution during the General Assembly's 62nd sessions in 2007 calling for a universal ban. The approval of a draft resolution by the Assembly's third committee, which deals with human rights issues, voted 99 to 52, with 33 abstentions, in favor of the resolution on 15 November 2007 and was put to a vote in the Assembly on 18 December.

Again in 2008, a large majority of states from all regions adopted a second resolution calling for a moratorium on the use of the death penalty in the UN General Assembly on 20 November. 105 countries voted in favor of the draft resolution, 48 voted against and 31 abstained.

A range of amendments proposed by a small minority of pro-death penalty countries were overwhelmingly defeated. It had in 2007 passed a non-binding resolution (by 104 to 54, with 29 abstentions) by asking its member states for "a moratorium on executions with a view to abolishing the death penalty. A number of regional conventions prohibit the death penalty, most notably, the Sixth Protocol (abolition in time of peace) and the 13th Protocol (abolition in all circumstances) to the European Convention on Human Rights. The same is also stated under the second Protocol in the American Convention on Human Rights, which, however has not been ratified by all countries in the Americas, most notably Canada and the United States. Most relevant operative international treaties do not require its prohibition for cases of serious crime, most notably, the International Covenant on Civil and Political Rights. This instead has, in common with several other treaties, an optional protocol prohibiting capital punishment its wider abolition.

Several international organizations have made the abolition of the death penalty (during time of peace) a requirement of membership, most notably the European Union (EU) and the Council of Europe. The EU and the Council of Europe are willing to accept a moratorium as an interim measure. Thus, while Russia is a member of the Council of Europe, and the death penalty remains codified in its law, it has not made use of it since becoming a member of the Council-Russia has not executed anyone since 1996. With the exception of Russia abolitionist it. Kazakhstan abolitionist for ordinary crimes only And Belarus. All European countries are classified as abolitionist

Mr. God , state or Republic of Justice does believe that death sentence in the earth is a punishment, because death was created by you Mr. God, we believe that death is a world road , what the reason to punish someone to death, when in fact the death is the option

The death penalty will be regarded as cruel and unusual punishment, everyone fears punishment, and everyone fears death, just as you do. Therefore you do not kill or cause to be killed

Execution of criminals and political opponents has been used by nearly all
societies, both to punish crime and to suppress political dissent. In most
places that practice capital punishment it is reserved for murder, espionage,
treason, or as part of military justice. In some countries sexual crimes, such
as rape, adultery, incest and sodomy, carry the death penalty, drug
trafficking is also a capital offense. In china, human trafficking and serious
cases of corruption are punished by the death penalty. In militaries around
the world courts-martial have imposed death sentences such as cowardice,
insubordination, and mutiny.

The use of formal execution extends to the beginning of recorded history,
most historical records and various primitive tribal practices indicate that the
death penalty was a part of their justice system. Communal punishment for
wrongdoing generally, included compensation by the wrongdoer, corporal
punishment, shunning, banishment and execution. Usually compensation or
bloods feuds.

A blood feud or vendetta occurs when arbitration between families or tribes
fails or an arbitration system is non-existent. This form of Justice was
common before the emergence of an arbitration system based on state or
organized religion. It may result from crime, land disputes or a code of honor.
Acts of retaliation underscore the ability of the social collective to defend it
and demonstrate to enemies that injury to property, rights, or the person will
not go unpunished. However, in practice, it is often difficult to distinguish
between a war of vendetta and one of conquest.

Severe historical penalties include breaking wheel, boiling to death, flaying,
slow slicing, disembowelment, crucifixion, impalement, and crushing,
stoning, execution by burning dismemberment, sawing, decapitation,
escapism, neck lacing or blowing from a gun, God close is eyes knowing that
human need God assistance.

Elaborations of tribal arbitration of feuds included peace settlements often
done in a religious context and compensation system. Compensation was
based on the Principe of substitution which might include material
compensation, exchange of brides or grooms, or payment of the blood debt.
Settlement rules could allow for animal blood to replace human blood, or
transfers of property or blood money or in some case an offer of a person for
execution. The person offered for execution did not have to be an original

perpetrator of the crime because the system was based on tribes, not individuals. Blood feuds could be regulated at meetings, such as the Viking things systems deriving from blood feuds may survive alongside more advanced legal systems or be given recognition by courts. One of the more modern refinements of the blood feuds is the duel.

In certain parts of the world, nations in the form of ancient republics, monarchies or tribal oligarchies emerged. These nations were often united by common linguistic, religious or family ties. Moreover, expansion of these nations often occurred by conquest of neighboring tribes or nations. Consequently, various classes of royalty, nobility, various commoners and slave emerged. Accordingly, the systems of tribal arbitration were submerged into a more unified system of justice which formalized the relation between the different classes, rather than "tribes". The earliest and most famous example is Code of Hammurabi which set the different punishment and compensation according to the different class/group of victims and perpetrators. The Torah (Jewish law), also known as the Pentateuch lays down the death penalty for murder, kidnapping, magic, violation of the Sabbath, blasphemy, and a wide range of sexual crimes, although evidence suggests that actual executions were rare.

Defendant God need to know that in many circumstance, never protect or assisted people in danger, include Juvenile offenders:

The death penalty for Juvenile offenders has become increasingly rare Considering the Age of Majority is still not 18 in some countries, since 1990 nine countries have executed offenders who were juveniles at the time of their crimes. The People's Republic of China, Democratic Republic of the Congo, Iran, Nigeria, Pakistan, Saudi Arabia, Sudan, the United States and Yemen.

Starting in 1642 within British America, an estimated 365 juvenile offenders were executed by the states and federal government of the United States. The United States Supreme Court abolished capital punishment for offenders under the age of 16 in Thompson v. Ockham (1988), and for all Juveniles in Roper v. Summons (2005). In addition, in 2002, the United States Supreme Court declared unconstitutional the executions of individuals with an intellectual disability, in Atkins v. Virginia.

Between 2005 and May 2008, Iran, Pakistan, Saudi Arabia, Sudan and Yemen were reported to have executed child offenders, the most being from Iran

Iran, despite its ratification of the Convention on the Rights of the Child and International Covenant on Civil and Political Rights, was the world's biggest executioner of juvenile offenders, for which it has received international condemnation, the country's record is the focus of the Stop Child Executions Campaign, But on 10 juvenile offenders will be sentenced on a separate law than of adults. Based on the Islamic law which now seems to have been revised, girls at the age of 9 and boys at 15 of lunar year (11 days shorter than a solar year) were fully responsible for their crimes.

Iran accounted for two-thirds of the global total of such executions has roughly 140 people on death row for crimes committed as juveniles. The past executions of Mahmoud Asgari, Ayaz Marhoni and Makwan Moloudzadeh became international symbols of Iran's child capital punishment and the judicial system that hands down such sentences.

Saudi Arabia executes criminals who were minors at the time of the offense. In 2013, Saudi Arabia was the center of an international controversy after it executed Rizana Nafeck, a Sri Lankan domestic worker, who was believed to have been 17 years old at the time of the crime.

Somalia, there is evidence that child executions are taking place in the parts of Somalia controlled by the Islamic Courts Union. In October 2008, a girl, Aisho Ibrahim Dhuhulow was buried up to her neck at a football stadium, then stoned to death in front of more than 1,000 people. The stoning occurred after she had allegedly pleaded guilty to adultery in a shariah court in Kismayo, a city controlled by the ICU. According to a local leader associated with the ICU, she had stated that she wanted shariah law to apply. However, other sources state that the victim had been crying, that she begged for merci and had to be forced into the hole before being buried up to her neck in the ground. Amnesty International later learned that the girl was in fact 13 years old and had been arrested by the al-Shabab militia after she had reported being gang-raped by three men.

Mr. God I believe without you, the earth will be better; you are a big problem in this planet, wrongful execution? How and when a leader may have intervened? When you are able to make a right decision to resolve all contradiction matter? Just believing in you dreaming? , think only for the last day? Think only for the end of the world?

It is frequently argued that capital punishment leads to miscarriage of justice through the wrongful execution of innocent persons. Many people have been proclaimed innocent victims of the death penalty.

Some have claimed that as many as 39 executions have been carried out in the face of compelling evidence of innocence or serious doubt about guilty from in the US from 1992 through 2004, newly

Available DNA evidence prevented the pending execution of more than 15 death row inmates during the same period in the US, but DNA evidence is only available in a fraction of capital cases.

However, since the death reinstatement in the United States during the 1970s, no inmate executed has been granted posthumous pardon.

Also improper procedure may result in unfair executions. For example, Amnesty International argues that in Singapore" the Misuse of Drugs Act contains a series of presumptions which shift the burden of proof from the prosecution to the accused. This conflicts with the universally guarantee right to be presumed innocent until proven guilty. This refers to a situation when someone is being caught with drugs. In this situation, in almost any jurisdiction, the prosecutor has a prima facie case.

Abolitionists argue that retribution is simply revenge and cannot be condoned. Others while accepting retribution as an element of criminal justice nonetheless argue that life without parole is a sufficient substitute. It is also argued that the punishing of a killing with another killing is a relatively unique punishment for a violent act, because in general violent crimes are not punished by subjecting the perpetrator to a similar act.

Non-Assistance of person in danger, negligence of Mr. God culpability, knowing that execution is not simply death; it is just a different from the privation of life as a concentration camp is from prison.

Most states believe that Capital punishment is a legal process whereby a person is put to death or the death is a normal symbol that nobody is this planet is able to escape, The earth had been sentenced to death, why put someone to death, when in fact, any time, any day, death will show up, Police, Judge, prosecutor, Parliament members both ignore that death is a normal symbol that Mr. God created?   Killing is not a solution, but God fail to prevent the earth by committed all executions

Prosecutor: Mr. God for all disasters that you created and the consequences, after review all references I will ask the Jury to find you guilty and sentence to death

Judge: Mr. Defense lawyer the court request you intervention

Defense lawyer: Thank you Judge, thank you Jury for all you attention in this matter, I'm very disappointed, very surprise that the Republic of Justice fail to know God power, fail to think that God is a loving., fail to understand that without God this Republic never exist, without God nobody will be in this planet, My Client is innocent to all charge that the State file against him, don't forget that God is the one created the earth, all that we have in this planet, he is the only can take away what we have, before we exist nobody known were we was, today the State of Justice file complaint against God and decided to brought God before Universal Tribunal Court, I believe someone lost is mind.

God created man in his own image, in the image of God he created him, male and female he created them, he told them to be fruitful and increase in number, fill the earth and subdue it, rule over the fish of the sea and the birds of the air and over every living creature that moves on the ground, then God told them "I give you every seed –bearing plan on the face of the whole earth and every tree that has the fruit with seed in it. They will be yours for food. And to all the beasts of the earth and all the births of the air and all the creatures that move on the ground, everything that has the breath of life in it, he give them green plant for food, there was evening, and there was morning.

Here, is how the State of Justice forget by filing accusation against Mr. God

The Fall of Man and all consequences that earth becomes   victims, death, storm, wars, diseases etc....

Now the serpent was craftier than any of the wild animals that God made, he said to the woman "Did God really say, "You must not eat from any tree in the garden?"

The woman said to the serpent, we may eat fruit from the trees in the garden, but God did say, you must not eat fruit from the tree that is in the middle of the garden, and you must not touch it, or you will die. "You will not surely die" the serpent said to the woman. God knew that when you eat of it your eyes will be opened, and you will be like God, knowing good and evil.

When the woman saw that the fruit of the tree was good for food and pleasing to the eye, and also desirable for gaining wisdom, she took some and ate it. She also gave some to her husband, who was with her, and he ate it, then the eyes of both of them were opened, and they realized they were naked, so they sewed fig leaves together and made coverings for themselves.

Then the man and his wife heard the sound of the God, and they hid from God among the trees of the garden, but God called to the man, where are you?

He answered, I heard you in the garden, and I was afraid because I was naked, so I hid

And he said, who told you that you were naked? Have you eaten the tree that I commanded you not to eat from?

The man said, The woman you put here with me, she gave me some fruit the tree, and I ate it, God said to the woman, what is this you have done?

The woman said "The serpent deceived me, and I ate"

My client God, told serpent , because you have done this, cursed are you above all the livestock and all the wild animals, you will crawl on your belly and you will eat dust all the days of your life, and I will put enmity between your offspring and hers, he will crush your head, and you will strike his heel

To the woman he said, I will greatly increase your pains in childbearing, with pain you will give birth to children. Your desire will be for your husband, and he will rule over you.

My client God told Adam, because you listened to your wife and ate from the tree about which I commanded you. You must not eat of it: Cursed is the ground because of you through painful toil you will eat of it all the days of your life. I will produce thorns and thistles for you and you will eat the plants of the field, by the sweat of your brow, you will eat your food until you return to the ground, since from it you were taken, for dust you are, and to dust you will return.

Defense lawyer: My Client God did the right thing, but the earth is responsible for all the crimes, all atrocities, without disobedience, the earth will be in the peace, After review all complaints against my Client God, You will never filed complaint against my Client by using speculation, You need to show by the evidence that my client committed the crimes and no by speculation

I will not spend too much times argued against the state, honorable Judge, Jury's, I didn't find any evidence that Client God is liable or guilty, I ask the Jury's to free my client to all charges, is not guilty for any crimes. Thank you Judge, thank you Jury's for all you times, thank you for no find my client guilty. Thank again.

Prosecutor: Honorable Judge, I have one witness that I need before I respond to the defense lawyer

Judge order the witness to appear in the court.

Gerard Donnchadh (Plaintiff against God):

Prosecutor: Please Mr. Donnachadh, swear under oath: Do you tell the truth, the whole truth and nothing but the truth?

Donnchdh: I do

Prosecutor: How old are you?

Donnchadh: I'm 65 years old

Prosecutor: Are you married?

Donnchadh: Yes, I'm married sir

Prosecutor: How long have you been married?

Donnchadh: I've been married 51 years

Prosecutor: How many Kids do you have?

Donnachadh: I have 6 kids 4 boys, 2 Girls

Prosecutor: Do you work Mr Donnachadh? And does your wife work too?

Donnachadh: Yes, I work as a truck driver and my wife works as a nurse

Prosecutor: Do you love you Kids?

Donnachadh: Off course sir, I love my kids from the button of my heart

Prosecutor: What makes your kids think you love them?

Donnachadh: We do the best to help them by working hard to provide food send them to school and spend quality time with them as much as possible.

Prosecutor: How you lost right leg?

Donnachadh: One day we went to ocean swimming, my son fallen in the bridge, so I decided to save my son, and I jumped, I hit in the rock and save my son, We went to hospital Doctor told that he can save my leg, he decided to cut my leg, but I'm still proud what I did, by save my son

Prosecutor: Do you want to tell me that you are loving father, who love kids?

Donnachadh: Yes, I love my kids

Prosecutor: You save you son, because you didn't want him to death?

Donnachadh: death is something normal, but I will not let happen, if you can prevent any accident, I will do

Prosecutor: Thank you Mr. Donnachadh

Prosecutor: Mr. Defense lawyer do you have any question to ask Mr. Donnachadh?

Defense lawyer: No thank you

Prosecutor: Mr. Lariviere, please come here, stay in front of the jury's

Lariviere; I sweat under oath to tell the truth and nothing but the truth.

Prosecutor: Thank you Mr. Lariviere

Prosecutor: how old are you?

Lariviere: I'm 50 years old

Prosecutor: Do you have a Job? What you level of education?

Lariviere: I'm scientist, I work in the laboratory, I' m specialist of kill Ant, Roach, include a different insects.

Prosecutor: Are you married?

Lariviere: Yes, I'm married father of 3 kids, two girls and one boy

Prosecutor: Do you love you kids?

Lariviere: Yes, I love my kids

Prosecutor: About you wife, did she work?

Lariviere: My wife work, she is a Doctor, in charge of chemical that produce acid

Prosecutor: Did you bring acid or bottle of roach to your house? To prevent any insects? When you brought this chemical to you house, did you expose in front of you kids?

Lariviere: We take this product very carefully, we keep very fare from kids, because this chemicals is very dangerous for kids, we don't expose

Prosecutor: You want to tell me that you expose chemical in front of kids it's not a good idea?

Lariviere: it's not a good idea, expose chemical in front of kids

Prosecutor: Why?

Lariviere: Because we don't want to lost them, If we make a mistake they will died, so this is the reason why we keep them far away from them, We love them, we parents, we have obligation to protect kids.

Prosecutor: Thank you Mr.lariviere

Prosecutor: Honorable Judge, Jury's, We hear the testimony of my plaintiffs, they show you love, love their families, the protects their kids, they don't want kids to be in trouble, one of my plaintiff, lost his leg because I went to save his son live, my plaintiffs scientists wife and husband never expose chemicals in front of kids, this way we call love, love means action, love is not just by talking. Mr. God lawyer fail to defend this guy, because he had not argument to convince jury that Mr. God is a loving father, no, is not

Let talk about Adam and Eve, Mr. God is a good player, who doesn't love people, this the reason he scared to be in public, Mr. God know the pass, he know the present, he know the future, by created Adam and Eve he pointed out a poison tree, knowing that Satan or serpent will deceive them, God play the games with serpent, finally he destroys their live, make them suffering, make them died, created different diseases, earthquakes, killing thousands people, Since God know that Adam and Eve will be attempted by serpent, why he didn't prevent that? Dear Jury do you believe this guy is able to control the earth, by doing stupid like that? My recommendation to you is to find him guilty and sentence him to death, the world will be in peace without this guy (God).

Judge: Thank you audience, thank you the State of Justice, thank you defense lawyer, the court had decided to send the jury in deliberation, Before deliberation, we will call Satan for all accusation that State of Justice file against him, we have a defense lawyer for Mr. Satan present in the Court.

Prosecutor: Honorable Judge, thank you. Mr. Satan the state of Justice charge you for Instigator, complicity in murders, atrocity, wars, rape, conspiracy with God against people in the earth.

The World was created by this guy next to you, there was no death, live was nice, you incite Adam and Eve to disobedience, they accepted what you told them, and the guy next to you decided to punish them, he made their life miserable, Animal becomes dangerous, everything become difficulties, the consequence of instigator made people in the earth suffering, by reading all complaining and all references that the court filed against God, your contribution or participation was at 40%, I will not explain over again, because the jury know that you the one started all disastrous , If you didn't excite Adam and Eve by violated the commandment of his powerfully leadership, the earth will have been in good condition, by accepted you stupidity, death, wars, rape, genocide, injustice, racists become the symbol of this planet. I will not spend too much time explain all accusation for the murders, diseases that world had been victimized, you culpability, include misconduct of religious leaders:

Catholic sex abuse case are a series of allegations, investigations, trials and convictions of child sexual abuse crimes committed by Catholic priests and members of Roman Catholic orders against children as young as three years old with the majority between the ages of 11 and 14. These cases include anal and oral penetration and have resulted in criminal prosecution of the abusers and civil lawsuits against the church's dioceses and parishes. Many of the cases span several decades and are brought forward years after the abuse occurred. Cases have also been brought against members of the Catholic hierarchy who did not report sex abuse allegations to the legal authorities. It has been shown they deliberately moved sexually abusive priests to other parishes where the abuse sometimes continued. This has led to a number of fraud cases where the church has been accused of misleading victims by deliberately relocating priest accused of abuse instead of removing them from their positions.

The cases received significant media and public attention in Canada, Ireland, the United States, and throughout the world. In response to the attention, members of the church hierarchy have argued that media coverage has been excessive and disproportionate. According to a Pew Research Center Study, media coverage mostly emanated from the United States in 2002, when the Boston Globe began a critical investigation. By 2010 much of the reporting focused on child abuse in Europe. From 2001-2010 the Holy See, the central governing body of the Catholic Church has considered sex abuse allegations concerning about 3,000 priests dating back up to 50 years, according to the Vatican Promoter of Justice. Cases worldwide reflect patterns of long term abuse and the covering up of reports. Church officials and academics knowledge about the Roman Catholic Church say that sexual abuse by clergy is generally not discussed, and thus is difficult to measure. In the Philippines, where as of 2002 at least 85% of the population is Catholic, revelations of child sexual abuse by priests followed the United States' reporting in 2002. Research and expert opinion reported in 2010 indicated that evidence does not point to men within the Catholic Church being more likely than others to commit abuse. Has indicated that, the prevalence of abuse by priests had fallen sharply in the previous 20 to 30 years.

Mr. Satan, you know all disasters that the world had been suffering, was caused by you, you are the first instigator for the misery of this planet, child abuse, wars, genocides, I can believe you misconduct to convince religious leaders abuse child? This leaders spend most of their times mobilized people to the right way, but you temptation brought them by committing sexual exploitation; the Republic of justice will never accept you misconduct.

In Northern Ireland (part of the United Kingdom of Great Britain and Northern Ireland, politically distinct from the Republic of Ireland) the largest inquiry in UK legal history into institutional sexual and physical abuse in institutions that were in charge of children from 1922 to 1995 was held, starting in January 2014? The De La Sale Brothers and sisters of Nazareth admitted early in the inquiry to physical and sexual abuse of children in institutions in Northern Ireland that they controlled, and issued an apology to victims. Not all the abuse being investigated by the inquiry is associated with Catholic institutions.

Norway: In April 2010, it was reported that former bishop of the Norwegian Catholic Church, George Muller, had confessed to the Norwegian Police in early January 2010 that he had sexually abused an underage altar boy 20 years earlier. The Norwegian Catholic Church was made aware of the incident but did not alert the authorities. Muller was made to step down as a bishop in July 2009.

Poland: In October 2013, the Catholic Church in Poland explicitly refused to publish data on sexual abuse, but said that, if the data were to be published, the scale would be seen to be very low. Bishop Antoni Dydycz said that priests should not be pressed to report sexual abuse to state authorities, invoking the ecclesiastical seal of confession which bans them from revealing what is said in the rite of confession. In November 2013 the Minister of Justice said that there were 1,454 persons in prisons for acts of pedophilia of whom one was a Catholic priest.

United States, which has been the lead focus of much of the scandals and subsequent reforms, Bishop Accountability.org, an "Online archive established by lay Catholics, reports that over 3,000 civil lawsuits have been filed against the church, some of these cases have resulted in multi-million dollar settlements with many claimants. In 1998 the Roman Catholic Diocese of Dallas paid $30.9 million to twelve victims of one priest. From 2003 to 2009 nine other major settlements involving over 375 cases with 1551 claimants/victims, resulted in payments over US$ 1.1 billion. The Associated Press estimated the settlements of sex abuse cases from 1950-2007 totaled more than 2billion. "BishoAccountability puts the figure at more than $3billion in 2012. Addressing a flood of abuse claims, five dioceses have declared bankruptcy due to sex abuse cases from 2004-2011.

Although bishops had been sending sexually abusive priests to facilities such as those operated by the Servants of the Paraclete since 1950.there was scant public discussion of the problem until the mid-1960. Even then, most of the discussion was help amongst the Catholic hierarchy with little or no coverage in the media. A public discussion of sexual abuse of minors by priests took place at a meeting sponsored by the National Association for Pastoral Renewal held on the campus of the University of, Notre Dame in 1967, to which all U.S. Catholic bishops were invited.

Various local and regional discussions of the problem were help by Catholic bishops in later years. It was not until the 1980 that discussion of sexual abused by Roman Catholic clerics began to be covered as a phenomenon in the news media of the United States. According to the Catholic News Service public awareness of the sexual abuse of children in the United States and Canada emerged in the 1970 and the 1980 as an outgrowth of the awareness of physical abuse of children. In 1981 Father Donald Roemer of the Archdiocese of Los Angeles pleaded guilty to felonious sexual of a minor. The case received widespread media coverage. In September 1983, the National Catholic Reporter published an article on the topic. The subject gained wider national notoriety in October 1985 when Louisiana priest Gilbert Gauthe pleaded guilty to 11 counts of molestation of boys. After the coverage of Gauthe's crimes subsided, the issue faded to the fringes of public attention until the mid-1990, when the issue was again brought to national attention after a number of books on the topic was published. In early 2002 the Boston Globe's Pulitzer winning coverage of sexual abuse cases involving Catholic priests drew the attention. First, of all the United States and ultimately the world, to the problem. Other victims began to come forward with their own allegations of abuse, resulting in more lawsuits and criminal cases. Since then, the problem of clerical abuse of minors has received significantly more attention from the church hierarchy, law enforcement agencies, government and the news media.

In 2003 Archbishop Timothy M. Dolan of the Roman Catholic Archdiocese of Milwaukee authorized payments of as much as US$20.000 to sexually abusive priests to convince them to leave the prieshood.

As recently as 2011 FrCurtis Wehmeyer was allowed to work as a priest in Minesota despite many people having reported concern about his sexual abusing two boys. After Wehmeyer's arrest there are complaints the responsible clergy were more concerned with how to spin in a favorable light than in helping victims.

Bishop-Accountability.org. an "online archive established by lay Catholics" reported that over 3,000 civil lawsuits have been filed against the church in the United States. Some of these cases involved many claimants and resulted in multi-million dollar settlements.

Jay Report: In the United States, John Jay Report commissioned and funded by the U.S. Conference of Catholic Bishops was based on volunteer surveys completed by the Roman Catholic dioceses in the United States. The 2004 John Jay Report was based on a study of 10.667 allegations against 4,392 priests accused of engaging in sexual abuse of a minor between 1950 and 2002.

The surveys filtered provided information from diocesan files on each priest accused of sexual abuse and on each of the priest victims to the research team, in a format which did not disclose the names of the accused priests or the dioceses where they worked. The dioceses were encouraged to issue reports of their own based on the surveys that they had completed. The report stated there were approximately 10,667 reported victims of clergy sexual abuse "between" 1950-2002.

Bishop Manuel D. Moreno of Tucson, Arizona, USA repeatedly to have two local abusive priests defrocked and disciplined, pleading unsuccessfully in a letter of April 1997 with Cardinal Joseph Ratzinger as head of the Congregation for the Doctrine of the Faith to have one of them, who was first suspended in 1990 and convicted by the church in 1997 of five crimes including sexual solicitation in the confessional, defrocked. The two were finally in 2004. Bishop Moreno had been heavily criticized for failing to take action until details of his efforts became public

In a New York Times article, Bishop Blasé J. Cupich, chairman of the United Bishops Committee for the Protection of Children and Young People, is quoted explaining why Father Fitzgerald's, views, by and large, were considered bizarre with regard to not treating people medically, but only spiritually, and also segregating a whole population with sexual problems on a deserted island, and finally, there was mounting evidence in the world of psychology that indicated that when medical treatment is given, these people can, in fact, go back to ministry. This was a view which Cupich characterized as one that the bishops came to regret. In 2010 several secular and liberal Catholics were calling for Pope Benedict XVI's resignation, citing the action of then Cardinal Ratzinger's blocking of efforts to remove a priest convicted of child abusive. The pope did eventually resign in 2013, although he stated that he did so because of his declining health.

In 2012, Monsignor William Lynn became the first United States church official to be convicted of child endangerment because of his part in covering up child sex abuse allegations by clergy. Lynn was responsible for making recommendations as to the assignment of clergy in the Archdiocese of Philadelphia. He was found guilty of one count of endangering the welfare of a child. On July 24, 2012, Lynn was sentenced to three to six years in prison

Secrecy among bishop, it was revealed that some bishops had facilitated compensation payments to victims on condition that the allegations remained secret, for example, according to the Boston Globe, the Archdiocese of Boston secretly settled child sexual abuse claims against at least 70 priests from 1992 to 2002. In November 2009, the Irish Commission to inquire into Child Abuse reported its findings in which it concluded that: the Dublin Archdiocese's pre-occupations in dealing with cases of child sexual abuse, at least until the mid-1990s, were the maintenance of secrecy, the avoidance of scandal, the protection of the reputation of the Church, and the preservation of assets. All other considerations, including the welfare of children and justice for victims, were subordinated to these priorities. The Archdiocese did not implement its own law rules and did its best to avoid any application of the law of the State.

In April 2010, Christopher Hitchens and Richard Dawkins wanted to prosecute the Pope for crimes against humanity due to what they see as his role in intentionally covering up abuse by priests. In a CNN interview a few day's later, however, Dawkins declined to discuss the international crime law courts definition of crime against humanity, saying it is a difficult legal question. In April 2010, a lawsuit was filed in the Milwaukee Federal Court by an anonymous "John Doe 16" against the Vatican and Pope Benedict XVI. The plaintiff accused Ratzinger and others of having covered up abuse cases to avoid scandal to the detriment of the concerned children. In February 2011, two suspicion, that Joseph Ratzinger, as head of the Congregation for the Doctrine of the Faith, covered up the sexual abuse of children and youths and protected the perpetrators.

Internal division became public, with Christopher Cardinal Schonborn accusing Cardinal Angelo Sodano of blocking Ratzinger's investigation of a high-profile case in the mid-1990s

In the trial of the French Bishop Pierre Pican, who received a suspended jail sentence for failing to denounce an abusive priest, the retired Cardinal Dario Castrillon Hoyos wrote a letter to support Pican in his decision. Exposed to heavy critiques Hoyos, claimed to have had the approval of Pope John Paul II

In 2011 Hoyos was heavily criticized again. This time the Congregation for the Clergy was blamed of having opposed in 1997 to the newly adopted rules of the Irish bishops, demanding the denouncement of every abusive priest to the police. The Archbishop of Dublin Diarmuid Martin described the cooperation with the Congregation for the Clergy as "disastrous"

Satan misconduct against priests, Satan influence makes Vatican denying responsibility (contrary to canon law).

The Vicar of Christ ... possesses full, immediate, and universal ordinary power in the Church, which he is always able to exercise freely. By virtue of his office, the Roman pontiff not only possesses power over the universal church, but also obtains the primacy of ordinary power over all particular churches and groups of them. A Vatican spokesman contradicted the canon law above stating. When individual institutions of national churches are implicated, does not regard the competence of the Holy See... The competence of the Holy See

Produced by a victim of clerical sex abuse for the British Broadcasting Corporation (BBC) in 2006, the documentary Sex Crimes and the Vatican included the claim that all allegations of sex abuse are to be sent to the Vatican rather than the civil authorities, and that "a secret church decree called' Crimen solicitations" imposes the strictest oath of secrecy on the child victim, the priest dealing with the allegation, and any witnesses. Breaking that oath means instant banishment from the Catholic Church excommunication. The documentary quoted the 2005 forms Report. A culture of secrecy and fear of scandal that led bishops to place the interests of the Catholic Church ahead of the safety of children.

Canon lawyer Thomas Doyle, who was included in the documentary as supporting the picture that it presented, later wrote with regard to the 1962 Crimen solicitations and the 2001 De delictis gravioribus as well as the Church's formal investigation into charges of abuse. There is no basis to assume that the Holy See envisioned this process to be a substitute for any secular legal process, criminal or civil. It is also incorrect to assume, as some have unfortunately done, that these two Vatican documents are proof of a conspiracy to hide to reform the Catholic Church that it was like: trudging through what can best be described as a swamp of toxic waste..

The Church was reluctant to hand over to the civil authorities' information about the Church's own investigation into charges. In the BBC documentary, Rick Romley, a district attorney who initiated an investigation of the Diocese of Phoenix, stated that the secrecy, the obstruction I saw during my unparalleled in my entire career as a DA. It was so difficult to obtain any information from the Church at all. He reported archives of documents and incriminating evidence pertaining to sex abuse that were kept from the authorities, which under the law could not be subpoenaed. The Church fails to acknowledge such a serious problem but more than that, it is not a passiveness but an openly obstructive way of not allowing authorities to try to stop the abuse within the Church. They fought us every step of the way.

There have been many debates over the causes of sex abuse cases, Satan had contributed more than Mr. God in priest's abuse cases, by inciting innocents' priests to child molestation

THE 2004 John Jay Report the problem was largely the result of poor seminary training and insufficient emotional support for men ordained in 1940s and 1950s. A report by the National Review issued simultaneously with the John Jay Report pointed to two major deficiencies on the part of seminaries, failure to screen candidates adequately, followed by failure to form these candidates appropriately for the challenges of celibacy. These themes are taken up by a recent memoir that combines a first –hand account of life in a minor seminary during the 1960s with a review of the scientific literature about sexually abusive behavior, and then identifies specific aspects of seminary life that could have predisposed future priests to engage in such behavior.

Some bishops and psychiatrists have asserted that the prevailing psychology of the times suggested that people could be cured of such behavior through counseling. Thomas Plante, a psychiatrist in abuse counseling and considered an expert on clerical abuse, states "the vast majority of the research on sexual abuse of minors didn't emerge until the early 1980s. So it appeared reasonable at the time to treat these men and them to their priestly duties. In hindsight, this was a tragic mistake.

Mr. Satan Lucifer, you misconduct make priests be involved in many crimes, fail to, spreading Mr. God messages, In 2005 article in the conservative Irish weekly the Western People proposed that clerical celibacy contributed to the abuse problem by suggesting that the institution of celibacy has created a "morally superior" status that is easily misapplied by abusive priests. The Irish Church's prospect of a recovery is zero for as long as bishops continue blindly to toe the Vatican line of Pope Benedict XVI that a male celibate priesthood is morally superior to other sections of society.

This view has been challenged and severely criticized by several scholars for denying the cases of nuns implicated in sexual abuse and pedophilia. In 1986, a history scholar from Stanford University, recovered archival information about investigation from 1619 to 1623 involving nuns in Vellano, Italy, secretly exploits illiterate nuns for several years. In 1998, a religious research national survey on revealed a very high number of nuns reporting childhood victimizations of sexual abuse by other nuns. It was further noted that the majority of nun-abuse victims are of the same sex.

In 2002, Markham examined the sexual histories of nuns to find several cases of nuns sexually abusing children. In the last decade, many more cases have been recovered suggesting that cases involving nuns are as frequent as or more frequent than those involving male priests

Satan inciting priests, nuns, by acting barbaric, it has been argued that shortage of priests caused the Roman Catholic hierarchy to act in such a way to preserve the number of clergy and ensure that sufficient numbers were available to serve their congregations despite serious allegations that some of these priests were unfit for duty. Others disagree and assert that the Church hierarchy's mishandling of the sex abuse cases merely reflected their prevailing attitude at the time towards any illegal activity by clergy. Author George Weigei, claims that it was the infidelity to orthodox Roman Catholic teaching, the "culture of dissent" of priests, women religious, bishops, theologians, Church bureaucrats, and activists who believed that the church proposed as true was actually false, was mainly responsible for this problem. Satan was to blamed by declining morals of the late 20th century as a cause of the high number of sexual abusive priests. The hypothesis that a purported decline in general moral standard was associated with an increase in abuse by clergy was promoted by a study by Jay College funded by the United States Conference of Catholic Bishops. The study claimed that the liberal 1960 caused the increase in abuse, and the conservative Reagan years led to its decline. Mr. Satan, let me explain you about Child sexual abuse, sexual offenses means Adult engages in sexual activity with a minor or exploits a minor for the purpose of sexual gratification, Republic of Justice argued that Children cannot consent to sexual activity with adults, and condemns any such action by an adult as a criminal and immoral act which never can be considered normal or society acceptable behavior. Only at the beginning of the 1900s did Western society begin to regard children as fledgling citizen whose creative and intellectual potential require fostering rather than cheap labor

Child was shaped by the same forces that shaped the rest of society: industrialization, urbanization, and consumerism. Child sex abuse has gained public attention in the past few decades and has become one of the most high profile crimes. Since the 1970s, child molestation and sexual abuse of children has increasingly been recognized has deeply damaging to children and thus unacceptable for society as a whole. While sexual use of children by adults has been present throughout history. It has only become the object of significant public attention in recent times. The first published work dedicated specifically to child sexual abuse appeared in France in 1857

In the 1950s, Gerald Fitzgerald, who founded the Congregation of the Servants of the Paraclete (a religious order that treats Roman Catholic priests who struggle with personal difficulties such as pedophilia). Concluded that (sexual abuse) offenders were unlikely to change and should not be returned to ministry, and this was discussed with Pope VI (1897-1978) and, "in correspondence with several bishops".

In 2001, sex abuse cases were first required to be reported to Rome. After 2002, revelation that cases of abuse were widespread in the Church, the results made public in 2004 showed that even after the public outcry, priests were moved out of the countries where they had been accused and were still in settings that bring them into contact with children. The cases received significant media and public attention in Canada, Ireland, the United States, and throughout the world. In response to the attention, members of the church hierarchy have argued that media coverage has been excessive and disproportionate. According to a Pew Research Center Study, media coverage mostly emanated from the United States in 2002, when a Boston Globe series began a critical mass of news reports, by contrast, in 2010 much of the reporting focused on child abuse in Europe.

Child sexual abuse became a public issue in the 1970s and 1980s. Prior to this point in time, sexual abuse remained rather secretive and socially unspeakable. Studies on child molestation were nonexistent until the 1920s and the first national estimate of the number of child sexual abuse cases was published in 1948, by 1968, 44 out of 50 U.S. states had enacted mandatory laws that required physicians to report cases of suspicious child abuse.

Second wave feminism brought greater awareness of child sexual abuse and violence against women, and made them public, political issues.

Legal action began to become more prevalent in the 1970s with the enactment of the Child Abuse Prevention and Treatment Act in 1974 in conjunction with the creation of the National Center on Child Abuse and Neglect. Since the creation of the Child Abuse Prevention and Treatment Act, reported child abuse cases have increased dramatically. The National Abuse Coalition was created in 1979 to create pressure in congress to create more sexual abuse laws.

Satan, inside priests and Child abuse influence:

In April, the Pontifical Academy for life organized a three-day conference, entitled "Abuse of Children and Young People by Catholic Priests and Religious, where eight non-Catholic psychiatric experts were invited to speak to near all Vatican dicasteries representatives. The panel of experts overwhelmingly opposed implementation of policies of "zero tolerance" such as was proposed by the U.S Conference of Catholic Bishops. One expert called such policies a "case of overkill" since they do not permit flexibility to allow for differences among individual cases.

In August Pope Benedict was personally accused in a lawsuit of conspiring to cover up the molestation of three boys in Texas by Juan Carlos Patino Arango in Archidiocese of Galveston-Houston. He sought and obtained immunity from prosecution as head of state of the Holy See. Some claimed that the immunity was granted after intervention by then US President George W. Bush. The Department of State recognized and allows the immunity of Pope Benedict XVI from this suit.

In November the Vatican published Criteria for the Discernment for person with Homosexual Tendencies, issuing new rules which forbid ordination of men with deep seated homosexual tendencies. While the preparation for this document had started ten years before its publication. This instruction is seen as an official answer by the Catholic Church to what was seen as a "pedophile priests" crisis.

Archbishop Csaba Ternyak, spoke about the way that the crisis had damaged the priests-bishops relationship. He noted that there was a "sense of gloom" felt by the overwhelming majority of priests who had been accused of any abuse but nonetheless who perceived that their bishops had turned against them and therefore had become disillusioned about the effectiveness of the laws of the Church to defend their dignity and their inalienable rights. Ternyak also noted that "there have been more than a few suicides among accused priests.

Why Satan destroys Church? Mr. Satan what make you incite priests abuse child? We, Republic of Justice, the rule of court don't tolerate Child abuse or Child molestation, the only sentence you will get "death sentence" zero tolerance Mr. Satan, and do you hear me?

Honorable Judge, we still have many references that Mr. Santan had been involve, he is the only "incite people by commit stupide misconduct, the World will never forgive this guy, Jury, is you obligation to take in consideration all references misconduct of priests, Mr. Satan , he is the first instigator, include the guy next to him (God).

In 2012, an Australian police report in the state of Victoria detailed 40 suicide deaths by people who had been abused by Catholic clergy. The Chief Commissioner of Victoria Police, in a submission to a parliamentary on the issue, recommended that some of the Church actions to hinder investigations be criminalized. In one diocese, a dedicated clergy abuse police strike force has laid more than 170 abuse charges. On 13 November, the president of the Australian Catholic Bishops Conference welcomed and promised cooperation with a Royal Commission, announced by the Prime Minister of Australia at the time, Julia Gillard, to broadly investigate child sexual abuse in institutions across Australia.

In November 2010, an independent group in Austria, that operates a hotline to help people exit the catholic Church released a report documenting physical, sexual, and emotional abuse perpetrated by Austrian priests, nuns, and other religious. The report is based on hotline calls 91 women and 234 men, who named 422 perpetrators of both sexes, 63% of whom were ordained priests.

Female victims of sexual abuse by Catholic priests tended to be younger than the males. Data analyzed by John Jay researchers, shows that the number and proportion of sexual misconduct directed at girls under 8 years old was higher than that experienced by boys the same age. A substantial number (almost 2000) of very young children were victimized by priests during this time period.

According to Donald Cozzens, by the end of the mid 1990s, it was estimated that more than half a billion dollars had been paid in jury awards, settlements and legal fees. This figure grew to about one billion dollars by 2002. Roman Catholics spent$615 million on sex abuse cases in 2007. As of March 2006, dioceses in which abuse was committed or in which abuse allegations were settled out of court had made financial settlements with the victims totaling over 1.5 billion. The number and size of these settlements made it necessary for the dioceses to reduce their ordinary operating expenses by closing churches and schools in order to raise the funds to make these payments. Several dioceses chose to declare Chapter 11 bankruptcy as a way to litigate settlements while protecting some church assets to ensure it continues to operate.

Many of the accused priests were forced to resign. Some priests whose crimes fell within statutes of limitation are in jail. Some have been defrocked. Others because they are elderly. Because of the nature of their offenses, or because they have had some success fighting the charges, cannot be defrocked under law. Dome priests live in retreat houses that are carefully monitored and sometimes locked.

Bernard Francis law, Cardinal and Archbishop of Boston, Massachusetts, United States resigned after Church documents were revealed which suggested he had covered up sexual abuse committed by priests in his archdiocese. On December 13, 2002 Pope John Paul II accepted law's resignation as Archbishop and reassigned him to an administrative position in the Roman Curia naming him archpriest of the Basilica di Santa Maggiore, and he later presided at one of the Pope's funeral masses. Law's successor in Boston, Archbishop Sean P. O'Malley found it necessary to sell substantial real estate properties and close a number of churches in order to pay the 120 million in claims against the archdiocese.

Two bishops of Palm Beach, Florida resigned due to child abuse allegations. Resigned bishop Joseph Keith was replaced by Anthony O'Connell, who later also resigned in 2002.

All the references stated above, The Republic of justice take in consideration Satan conspiracy against innocents priests, The poor priests spend thousand years in seminary studying theology to help the society, but Mr. Instigator destroys all their future, Satan his a myth, in this society, without Satan, priests will never abuse child, Please, my recommendation to the Jury is to find Satan guilty to all charges filed against him.

Prosecutor: Honorable Judge, Defense lawyers, Jury, the state of justice present to this audience the list of Satan ritual abuse allegations:

In 1999, two journalists from the Sun Herald claimed to have seen evidence of the child abuse of children. They interviewed six mothers whose children had disclosed experiences of SRA and organized abuse in New South Wales. The children's disclosures were corroborating, although, they had never met one another, and they had been able to draw representations of Satanic, ritual sites which were similar to ritual sites uncovered by police on the central coast of New South Wales. One mother stated her sons remembered being drugged and hypnotized. He said they dressed in black robes and had eye and mouth pieces cut out, she said, I know they're pretty dangerous people. I have had warnings outside the house telling me to stop investigations. We're fearful for our lives. The boys never want me out of their sight.

Belgium: During the investigation of a Belgian serial killer Marc Dutroux, a number of woman approached police claiming to be adult survivors of a network of sexual offenders. One witness described satanic ceremonies with a goal of disorienting new victims, causing them to doubt the reality of their memories and prevent disclosure.

Canada: One of the earliest claims of SRA was made in the book Michelle Remembers co-written by Canadian psychiatrist Lawrence Pazder and Michelle Smith, later Pazder's wife. The book detailed a Satanic cult that allegedly operated in Vatican, British Columbia.

The Martensville satanic sex scandal occurred in Martensville, Saskatchewan in 1992, where an allegation of day care sexual abuse hysteria escalated into claims of satanic ritual abuse.

Ireland: In 2007, a jury at Dublin Country's court unanimously ruled that an infant found stabbed to death over three decades ago was the daughter of Cynthia Owen. The infant was alleged to have been murdered by the infant's grandmother. The Minister of Justice had previously rejected a request by Cynthia Owen to have the body of the child exhumed, a decision Ms. Owen did not contest. The inquest was prohibited from assigning blame due to the Coroners Act of 1962 and therefore returned an open verdict. Also the jury was instructed that the standard of proof was not the "beyond a reasonable doubt "benchmark of criminal trials", but rather the lesser standards of determining whether Owen's claims were true based on the balance of probabilities. Ms. Owen made claims about a stillborn second child buried in the family garden, but police found no human remains after digging up the plot. During the trial, Owen provided her account of incest, organized abuse, and satanic ritual abuse orchestrated by her parents involving at least nine other men and her account was supported by her psychologist. She claimed that her brother, Michael, and sister, Theresa, were also abused, a charge that was denied by her older brother and father. One of the alleged abusers is Cynthia Owen's older brother, Peter Murphy Junior, while the father, Peter Murphy Senior, is also an alleged abuser, Michael, disappeared in 2002 and Sister Theresa's testified at the trial, stating that Theresa had spoken to him at length about her sexual abuse in childhood. Theresa Murphy committed suicide on February 24, 2005 as a result of childhood sexual abuse; this finding was supported by police evidence. Theresa was the child of her older sister, Margaret Murphy

Following the findings of the coroner's Court, Owen has raised questions regarding the disposal of her daughter's body and the failure of the police to investigate the murder. In particular, she has highlighted the fact that no blood or tissue samples were kept, that the bag and sanitary towels found alongside the murdered child have gone missing, that the records of the first inquest into the murder have gone missing, and that her daughter was buried in a mass grave alongside other infants. Owen claimed that the police knew about the murder and did nothing. She also stated that she felt robbed of justice by her mother's natural and peaceful death.

Owen's father, Peter Murphy Senior, and three of her sisters won the right to appeal the findings of the inquest from the High Court. The family claimed that the coroner was biased toward Owen, shielded her when giving evidence and was selective in the evidence presented to the jury. The case of murdered child was reported in 2008, and in 2013, to be the subject of an ongoing investigation by the Garda Siochana. A petition calling for further investigation received 10,256 signatures and was submitted to government authorities on April 3, 2014.

Italy: In 1998, six adults in Emilia-Romagna were arrested with allegations of prostituting their children and the production of child pornography. The children were also reported to be involved in satanic rituals. In 2002, four people were arrested for Satanism and paedophilia in Pescara.believed that the group may have abused dozens of children in rituals involving body's stolen ceremonies. In April 2007, six people were arrested for sexually abusing children in Rignamo Flamingo. The suspects were accused of filming the children in sexual acts with satanic overtones.

The Nertherlands: In 1989 a group of parents published allegations in a conservative magazine that their children had witnessed SRA and had been ritually abused from May, 1987 until October 1988 in Oude Pekela, a city in the north-eastern province of Groningen, the Netherlands. During the initial investigation, only the non-ritual aspects were reported in the press and investigated by the authorities and the allegations were unconfirmed. In 1989 the conservative Christian news program Tijdsein reported allegations that included satanic ritual abuse, to which there was no official response. After attending a conference in which the concept of satanic ritual abuse was discussed, Oude Pekela general practitioners Fred Jonker and Ietje Jonker-Bakker alleged that several children had been abused by unknown men in the context of satanic rituals. This was first reported in a lecture at the Institute of Education of London University and later published in several academic journals in both English and Dutch, but their findings were heavily criticized by American and Dutch scholars. National authorities were informed in 1991 and 1992 of the allegations, though no action was taken until the press was informed. The State Secretary of Justice responded to the allegations by appointed the Werkgroep Ritueel Misbruik multidisciplinary workgroup to study SRA in the Netherlands, which produced a report in 1994. The report concluded that it was unlikely SRA had occurred or the allegations were factually true, suggested the allegations were a defense mechanism produced in part by suggestive questioning by believing therapists, and that the stories were contemporary legends dispersed through a network of therapists and patients who were concerned with dissociative identity disorder.

South Africa: In 1990, Gert van Rooyen and his accomplice were accused of murdering several young girls, ultimately committing suicide while running from the police. One of the accused's sons was later himself accused of murdering a Zimbabwean girl in 1991, the same son claimed his father's victims were involved in international child pornography rings, slavery and Satanism rituals, but no evidence of this was found. The case was so similar to crimes committed by Marc Dutroux that multiple agencies investigated a possible international smuggling ring in prostituted children and body parts.

United Kingdom: There have been a number of cases in the United Kingdom in which SRA has been alleged. Some of the cases have garnered significant media attention, and they are listed below.

The National Society for the Prevention of Cruelty to Children documents of rituals abuse in 1990, with the publication of survey findings that, of 66 child protection teams in England, Wales and Northern Ireland, 14 teams had received reports of rituals abuse children and seven of them were working directly with children who had been ritually abused, sometimes in groups of 20. An investigation into SRA allegations by the British government produced over two hundred reports, of which only three were substantiated and proved to be examples of pseudo satanic, in which sexual abuse was the actual motivation and the rituals were incidental.

Cleveland: The Cleveland child abuses scandal featured allegations of SRA.

Rochdale: In 1990 there was a case in Rochdale which around twenty children's were removed from their homes by social services who alleged the existence of SRA after discovering satanic indicators. No evidence was found of satanic apparatus, and charges were dismissed when a court ruled the allegations were untrue. The children were removed from their homes sued the city council in 2006 for compensation and an apology.

Orkney: In 1990-1991 nine children of being sexually abused by their families and an alleged child abuse ring were removed by social services in Orkney. The abuse was also alleged to involve ritualistic elements. The parents approached the media and made the case national and international news. In

April 1991, a sheriff ruled that the evidence was seriously flawed and the children were returned home.

Mr. Satan, nothing make you think that one day you will not brought to the court because of stupidity that people had been criminalized?

Satan misconduct:

In June social services appealed the sheriff's ruling, but the appeal was overturned and an official inquiry was established in August 1991, which after 9 month's investigation at a cost of 6million, published its report in October 1992. It described the dismissal of the first judgment as most unfortunate and criticized all those involved, including the social workers, the police, and the Orkey Islands Councils, Social worker's training, methods, and judgment were given special condemnation, and the report stated that the concept of ritual abuse was not only unwarrantable at present but may affect the objectivity of practitioners and parents. A 1994 government report based on three years of research found that there was no foundation to the many claims of Satanic abuse.

Broxtone: In October 1987 children were removed from their families in Nottingham, and in February 1989 a Broxtowe family was charged with multigenerational child sexual abuse and neglect. A 600-page report on the incident concluded that there was no evidence of the SRA claims made by children or corroborating adults. Though the children may have been sadistically terrorized, allegations of organized satanic abuse were found to be baseless and the indicators used by the Social Services were without validity.

Lewis: In 2003 allegations by three children in lewis, Scotland resulted in the arrest of eight people for sexual abuse occurring between 1990 and 2000. A 2005 investigation by the Social Work Inspection Agency found extensive evidence of sexual, physical and emotional abuse and neglect. Police investigation resulted in allegations of an island-wide" Satanic pedophile ring", though charges were dropped nine months later following an inconclusive investigation.

A key witness who had implicated her family in the abuse and whose evidence was" vital" to the case of satanic abuse recanted her testimony in

2006 and the media raised questions about the nature of the police interviewing techniques. With a police spokesperson replying that the witness was questioned appropriately and that allegations were made by numerous witnesses.

Kidwelly:

In March 2011, four adults who lived in a cul-de-sac in the Welsh town of Kidwelly were convicted of multiple sex offenses against children and young, adults. The group led by Colin Batley was described by the media as a satanic sex cult, a quasi-religious sex cult and a pedophile cult. Members of the cult were initiated in a ceremony involving sex with an adult, and they were threatened with being killed if they did not take part in the ceremony, some of the victims were forced into prostitution. The prosecution said they practiced free sex and were influenced by Aleister Crowley. They dressed in hoods and read from Crowley's The Book of the Law, and some victims were made to wear inverted crosses.

United States: In the United States, major allegations of Satanic ritual abuse occurred in the Kern County child abuse cases, McMartin preschool trial and the West Memphis 3, which garnered word-wide media coverage. It was eventually determined that no satanic abuse ever took place in these cases due to false testimony and police misconduct.

Jordan, Minnesota: The first such case occurred in Jordan, Minnesota, in 1983, where several children made allegations against an unrelated man and their parents. The man confessed and then identified a number of the children's parents as perpetrators. Ultimately twenty four adults were charged with child abuse though only three went to trial with two acquittals and one conviction. Despite strong medical finding of sexual assault, all other charges were dropped after the young child witnesses decompensated under the duress of the criminal trial.

During the investigation, the children made allegations regarding the manufacturing of the child pornography, ritualistic animal sacrifice, coprophagia, urophagiaand infanticide, at which point the Federal Bureau of Investigation was alerted. No criminal charges resulted from the FBI investigation, and infanticide, at which point the Federal Bureau of Investigation was alerted. No criminal charges resulted from the FBI investigation, and in his review of the case, the Attorney General noted that the initial investigation by the local police and county attorney was so poor that it had destroyed the opportunity to fully investigate the children's allegations.

Judge Antonin Scalia referred to the Minnesota case in his summation on a later case, and stated, here is no doubt that some sexual abuse took place in Jordan, but there is no reason to believe it was as widespread as charged, and cited the repeated, well-intentioned but coercive techniques used by the investigators as damaging to the investigation. The bizarre allegations of the children, the ambiguities of the investigation and the unsuccessful prosecutions were widely covered by the media. A number of accused parents confessed to sexually abusing their children, received immunity, and underwent treatment for sexual abuse, while parental rights for six other children in the case were terminated.

Evidence: The evidence for SRA was primarily in the form of testimonies from children who made allegations of SRA, and adults who claim to remember abuse during childhood, that may have been forgotten and recovered during therapy. With both children and adults, no corroborating evidence has been found for anything except pseudosatanism in which the satanic and ritual aspects were secondary to and used as a cover for sexual abuse. Despite this lack of objective evidence, and aided by the competing definitions of what SRA actually was, proponents claimed SRA was a real phenomenon throughout the peak and during the decline of the moral panic. Despite allegations appearing in the United States, Holland, Sweden, New Zealand and Australia, no material evidence has been found to corroborate allegations of organized cult-based abuse that practices human sacrifice and cannibalism. Though trauma specialists frequently claimed the allegations made by children and adults were the same, in reality the statements made by adults were more elaborate, severe, and featured more bizarre abuse. In 95% of the adults' cases, the memories of the abuse were recovered during psychotherapy.

For several years, a conviction list assembled by believes the children advocacy group was circulated as proof of the truth of satanic ritual abuse allegations, though the organization itself no longer exists and the lists itself is egregiously out of date.

Two investigations were carried out to assess the evidence for SRA, In the United States; evidence was reported but was based on a flawed methodology with an overly liberal definition of a substantiated case. In the United Kingdom, a government report produced no evidence of SRA, but several examples of false Satanists faking rituals to frighten their victims.

United States: David Finkelhor completed and investigation of Child sexual abuse in daycares in the United States, and published a report in 1988. The report found 270 cases of sexual abuse, of which 36 were classified as substantiated cases of ritual abuse. Mary de Young has pointed out the report's definition of substantiated was overly liberated as it required only that one agency had decided that abuse had occurred, even it no action was taken, no arrests made, no operating licenses suspended. In addition, multiple agencies may have been involved in each case, with wide differences in suspicion and confirmation, often in disagreement with each other. Finkelhor, upon receiving a confirmation, would collect information from whoever was willing or interested to provide it and did not independently investigate the cases, resulting in frequent errors in their conclusions. No data is provided beyond case studies and brief summaries. Three other cases considered corroborating by the public. The McMartin preschool trial, a pre-school in County Walk, Florida and the murders in Matamoros, by Adolfo Constanzo, ultimately failed to support the existence of SRA. The primary witness in the Country Walk case repeatedly made, then withdrew ritually sacrificed by a drug gang inspired by the film "The Believer", but did not involve children or sexual abuse. The McMartin case resulted in no convictions and was ultimately based on accusation by children with no proof beyond their coerced testimonies. A 1996 investigation of more than 12,000 allegations of satanic, ritual and religious resulted in no cases that were considered factual or corroborated.

United Kingdom: A British study published in 1996 found 62 cases of alleged ritual abuse reported to researchers by police, social and welfare agencies from the period of 1988 to 1991. Representing a tiny proportion of extremely high-profile cases compared to the total number investigated by the agencies. Anthropologist Jean la Fontane spend several years researching ritual abuse cases in Britain at the behest of the government Producing several reports and the 1998 book Speak of the Devil, after reviewing cases reported to police and children protective services throughout the county, La

Fontane concluded that the only rituals she uncovered were invented by child abusers to frighten their victims of justify the sexual abuse. In addition, the sexual abuse occurred outside of the rituals, indicating the goal of the abuser was sexual gratification rather than ritual or religious. In cases involving satanic abuse, the satanic allegations by younger children were influenced by adults, and the concerns over the satanic aspects were found to be compelling due to cultural attraction of the concept, but distracting from the actual harm caused to the abuse victims.

Patient allegations: The majority of adult's testimonials occurred as a result of adults undergoing psychotherapy, in most cases therapy designed to elicit memories of SRA. Therapists claimed the pain expressed by the patients, internal consistency of their stories and similarity of allegations by different patients was evidence for SRA, but despite this, the disclosures of patients never resulted in any corroboration. Allegations of alleged victims that were obtained from mental health practitioners lacked verifiable evidence, were anecdotal and involved incidents that were years or decades old. The concern for therapists revolved around the pain of their clients, which is for them more important than the truth of their patient's statements. A sample of 29 patients in a medical clinic reporting SRA found no corroboration of the claims in medical records or in discussion with family members, and a survey of 2709 American therapists found the majority of allegations of SRA came from only sixteen therapists, suggesting that the determining factor in a patient making allegations of SRA was the therapist's predisposition. Further, the alleged similarities between patient accounts turned out to be illusory upon review, with adults describing far more elaborate, severe and bizarre abuse than children. Bette Bottoms, who reviewed hundreds of claims of adults and child abuse, described the ultimate evidence for the abuse as astonishingly weak and ambiguous, particularly given the severity of the alleged abuse. Therapists however, were found to believe patients as the allegations became more bizarre.

Welcome to the most critically judgment in the earth, ladies and Gentlemen, We Republic of Justice had filed complaint against Mr. God and Mr. Satan Lucifer.

Non assistance of person in danger:

The Arab Slave Trade

In the 8th century, Arabs had extended their domination in the eastern side Of Africa bordering the Indian Ocean they had built cities today buried under the Tropical forests regrowth by the Portuguese at the end of the 15th century who Toured the continent, they soon recovered, and two hundred years later, was again Become the masters of the coast.

At exactly what time Arabs entered Africa? It is difficult to answer but this sad Trade over millennia is estimated to have taken more than ten millions Africans via The Eastern route to India, Saudi Arabia and Turkey and also via the Trans Saharan Route to North Africa and the Mediterranean where in slave market such as Morocco, Africans were purchased to work as servant. Slaves were owned in all Islamic Societies sedentary and nomadic, ranging from Arabia in the centre, to North Africa in the West and to what is now Pakistan and Indonesia in the East.

During the 18th century, the Arab slave trade took a brutal turn. By 1839 Slaving became the prime Arab enterprise. The demand of slave of Saudi, Egypt and Persia created a wave of destruction on Eastern Africa. 45000 slaves Were passing through Zanzibar every year. To satisfy this demand, the Arabs Hunted deep into the interiors of Africa. They were following ancient trails from Bagamoyo, Kilwa, and Tanga where terror and destruction followed in their wake.

The Arabs plunders met with savage resistance which meant that the trade had a very high mortality rate. Many documents speak of the road littered with the weak and the dying, they abandoned and they maimed, left with yokes around their necks. Many as in the case of Tsavo became food for lions. Children who became a burden to the coffle gang were brutally murdered in front of their mothers

When Islam arrived, war and servitude were features of African and Arabian Life. Judaism existed among certain Arab tribes as well as Christianity, and like them Islam did not blatantly outlaw slavery; Islam did however blatantly outlawed chattel enslavement. The Quran with every reference to slavery ask the believer to free the slave as atonement for sin, the term "emancipating a slave and feeding an orphan" are repeated constantly throughout the Quran as acts which gain God's favor. Also there were regulations which enhanced the pre-Islamic laws with respect to the treatment of enslaved people. They were entitled to good care, to the same clothing and food as their masters.

Under Arab slavery men were castrated and the women were used as sex machines,

so that over generations the offspring of the enslaved women merged

into general Arab society, albeit into an inferior caste-type class of sub-species.

Today we have slave descendants across the Sahara, such as the Haran tines in

Mauritania, to the ebony blacks in Arabia. At this period, Black Africans were

Transported to the Islamic empire across the Sahara to Morocco and Tunisia from

West Africa, from Chad to Libya, along the Nile from East Africa, and up the

Coast of East Africa to the Persian Gulf. This trade had been well entrenched for

Over 600 years before Europeans arrived, and had driven the rapid expansion of

Islam across North Africa.

By the time of the Ottoman Empire, the majority of slaves were obtained by

raiding in Africa. Russian expansion had put an end to the source of "exceptionally

beautiful" female and "brave" male slaves from the Caucasians -- the women

were highly prized in the harem, the men in the military. The great trade networks

across North Africa were as much to do with the safe transportation of slaves as

Other goods. An analysis of prices at various slave markets shows that eunuchs

fetched higher prices than other males, encouraging the castration of slaves before

Export.

Ronald Segal in his book Islam's Black Slaves: The Other Diaspora explains

That the Islamic slave trade began some eight centuries before the Atlantic trade

And was conducted on a different scale providing slaves more often for domestic

- including sex - and military service. . An interesting point made by Segal in an

Interview was that "whereas the gender ratio of slaves in the Atlantic trade was

Two males to every female, in the Islamic trade it was two females to every male.

Despite the practice of enslaving Africans was made illegal in most of the

Western world in the 19th century. In the Middle East, however, under the Muslim

Ottoman Empire, it persisted. In the area later to be called Palestine, there was an

Apartheid society of slave owners. Although Africans have been in Palestine for

Centuries, most people know little about this migration. For centuries, under the

Ottoman Empire and before, slaves were brought from Africa. Some older people today remember stories told by their parents or grandparents of how they came to

be in Palestine. Therefore it is possible to discover something of the later history

of slavery. Several people mentioned that they had heard that there was a big

slave market in Egypt. Most people with any idea of where their ancestors came

from mention Sudan or Ethiopia. Sometimes they know the name of the town.

Indeed, it is probable that many Africans came from these countries as they are

near to Palestine. According to history books, slave traders and owners used to

make a distinction between Ethiopians (Habash) and other Africans such as the

Zanj from the East African Coast. In their racist way of thinking, they considered

the Ethiopians to be superior to the other Africans. Africans were called "Abed"

- which literally means slave. White and black slaves were separated, and there

were degrees of inferiority among African slaves as well.

1442

Europeans in their quest for less expensive labor have targeted blacks for

their strength and endure. In 1512, a treaty of trade and assistance was proposed by the King of Portugal to King Alfonso (king of Congo) who accepted it.

Indeed, African leaders had used to give prisoners of war to their friends, and the

Portuguese funded these prisoners inexpensive for their plantations and mines in

America.

The island of Sao Tome, colonized in 1490, became the rallying point of all

slaves. Young Africans sent to study in Portugal has never reached destination.

From Sao Tome, slaves departed for plantations in Brazil.

How the slave trade began in Portugal? In 1442, Antonio Goncalves and

Chamberlain landed on the African coast and brought ten slaves. In 1444, Lagos

Lanzarotte brought back two hundred and sixty three slaves and sells them easily.

The Portuguese was motivated to prove they had arrived in the land of blacks and

to satisfy their curiosity. In addition, Portuguese brought ivory, gold dust, Arabic

gum, and all sold in Lagos and Lisbon. In 1550, one tenth of the population of

Lisbon was composed of black slaves. America had become a Spanish domain.

The Inca and Aztec civilizations had been brutally beheaded on the highlands,

while on the coastal plain people less evolved was enslaved to plantation works.

The mortality was appalling in this community. To this end, the missionary

Las Casas came to plead their cause in Europe and proposed to replace them with

blacks, more robust, tractable, and acclimated to the tropics. Las Casas imagined

that blacks can buy their right to baptism and the salvation of their souls by the

easement of their body. The economic conditions was such as human greed had

quickly made the connection between the immense needs of the cheap labor of

the west ocean and the pool no less great of African people, in front of firearms

of European slavers. And this was the great gateway to the bottomless pit the U.S.

market.

When in 1485, Diego Cao sailed up the estuary from the river to the first

cataract, he made contact with local populations and meet with Mbanza Ngungu

the head of the Nzinga dynasty at Kuvu, a treaty of friendship was signed between

Congolese chiefs and King John II of Portugal. King Mani Congo requests that

Portugal sent missionaries, carpenters and masons. Youth are sent to Portugal to

study. Europe of the 15th century is in full economic development, so they must

find a land or naval way to reach India, along the African coast. The aim was to reconnect with India to do business.

Europeans had also intended to evangelize Africans. In 1491, the first

Catholic missionaries arrived, who immediately succeeded in converting King

Mani Congo; he is baptized and took the name João I, the city of Mbanza
Ngungu

became San Salvador. Mani Congo's son succeeded him in 1506; he took the

name of Alfonso 1. Congo has all the characteristics of a Christian kingdom,

missionaries settled in various places, churches are built, young people are

educated in the Portuguese school, the son of the King, Don Henry became
the

first bishop of the kingdom of Congo. Unfortunately, the commercial
advantages

granted to foreign favor slavery.

In 1454, Pope Nicolas V had spent the Portuguese monopoly on the African

coast and frictions occurred with Spain already based in the Canaries. Pope

Alexander VI settled the conflict by taking on the world map a meridian line,
one

hundred leagues west of Spain at the most extreme of the Azores. To the
west of

that line, everything came back to Spain and the Eastern area to Portugal. To
deal

of To Desillas in 1494 confirmed the papal verdict that put Africa in the
pocket

of Portugal.

King Francois the 1st of France wondered why it is excluded from the division of the world. Other European states did not consider this arbitrary

division. Protestants did not feel concerned the division of the world by Pope

Alexander VI.

1482 - The Arrival of Diego Cao in the Congo

For

centuries, Europeans knew nothing about Africa. In the 14th century, European sailors

sought routes to trade with India.

The Portuguese had reached the Congo estuary in 1482. In 1489 the Kingdom

of Congo ruler, Manikongo (Nzinga Nkuma), formed a trading agreement with

them, and missionaries and artisans were sent out from Portugal. These carpenters,

masons, stock-breeders, etc., were heavily involved in the re-development of the

Congolese capital, previously known as Mbanza Congo, which was now renamed

São Salvador.

Manikongo was succeeded by his son Alfonso (Nzinga Mbemba), who ruled

from 1506 to 1543. He modeled his court after that of Lisbon (creating Dukes,

Marquises, and Counts, mostly from family members). Members of his royal court

wore European dress. The Congo court spent a considerable fortune importing fabric, wine, and luxury items, the money obtained from the sale of slaves and

minerals. Slaves were obtained by Alfonso through border skirmishes with the

Loango (to the north), Ndongo (to the south), and Mbangala (further inland), and

through tribute collections. Although the Portuguese showed considerable interest

in the Congolese mining operations, Alfonso managed to maintain a monopoly on

production.

Although the Portuguese tried to restrict the Congo's access to other

markets (the Gold Coast and even Europe itself) by refusing to sell him ships, the

Kingdom of Congo maintained a small maritime presence at the port of Mpinda.

King Alfonso even 'owned' a couple of plantations on the island of São Tomé,

operated by two members of the royal household.

Exactly in 1482 when Diego Cao was heading with three ships to the southern

Atlantic Ocean to examine the African coast. He arrived in a place where the water

was turbulent, and where a lot of tree trunks were floating. He realized that he was

at the mouth of a great river: the River Congo. He directed his ships to the river and landed on the shore, where he erected a stone column of 2 and a half meters

high surmounted by a cross, he put his name, the name of the king of Portugal and

the date of his arrival. Diego Cao returned to Portugal, but returned three years

later and made the acquaintance of the population and King Nzinga Ntinu of Kivu

region, who became a friend of the Portuguese. He tried to ascend the river with its

boats, but he was arrested by the cataracts near the present town of Matadi.

At the point where they arrived, they engraved on stone in Portuguese: here

were landed ships of the King of Portugal. You can still read the entries today.

Friendly relations were established between the kingdom of Congo and Portugal,

missionaries introduced Christianity and traders settled in the country especially

along the Atlantic coast.

The business occupancy Bas-Congo was then realizes that time; unfortunately

it was accompanied by all kinds of abuses that made her unpopular. Missionary

works turned precarious. Without doubt, the king of the Congo was baptized in

1491; his grand- son became the first Congolese bishop in 1518.

Under the reign of King Bernardo I, difficulties arose between Portuguese and Congolese. Bernado sought the friendship from Dutch [Netherlands] who will

help him to drive the Portuguese. Those latter then, had to withdraw to Angola.

Soon, foreign traders bought from the Bantu Kings prisoners of war, and resell

them to browsers that transported them to America. Thus began the sad slave

trade.

However, the slave strut was less serious in Congo than some areas of Africa.

Before the arrival of the first Europeans in Africa, Arabs had already started this

process several centuries earlier.

The island of São Tomé was discovered by the Portuguese in 1472 - part of

the expanding European search for a route to the East, a source of suitable land to

colonize for wheat, vine and sugar production, and access to the legendary gold

mines of West Africa. In 1493 Alvaro Caminha was granted the right to create

a settlement on São Tomé (and begin plantations) by the Portuguese crown. In

1522, São Tomé came under direct Portuguese administration.

Initially settled by Portuguese overseers and convict laborers, São Tomé's

climate proved unsuitable for European workers and an alternative workforce

was needed. As the Portuguese extended their reach along the West African coast, they came into contact with Islamic slave traders who bought slaves in

West African for their trans-Saharan market. Although the Portuguese at that time

were predominantly interested in trading textiles, horses, tools, wine, and copper

for gold, pepper, and ivory, a small but significant market developed for African

slaves for São Tomé (as well as the other newly discovered islands along Africa's

Atlantic coast: Madeira, the Canary Islands, and Cape Verde Islands).

1516

During the first 15 years of the sixteenth century, slave exports to these islands

totaled around 2,500 a year. From 1516 to 1521 the number of slaves transported

rose to around 5,400 per year. This wasn't, however, due to an increased demand

for slaves on the various plantation islands - it was the result of a developing

slave trade from the Kingdom of Congo, further down the Atlantic coast, and

the discovery that a profit could be made selling slaves to the Islamic traders

along Africa's Gold Coast. São Tomé became a transit point for traders taking

slaves from the Congo for sale in the Gold Coast and to the other Portuguese

plantation islands (a few hundred each year were even taken back to Portugal

itself). Between 1510 and 1540, four to six slave ships continually transported slaves from São Tomé to the Gold Coast. The smaller caravels could carry 30 to

80 slaves; the larger vessels could carry between 100 to 120 slaves at a time.

Slave exports to the Americas began in the 1530s, and by 1550 the majority

of the passing trade was destined for the Spanish Caribbean. The trans-Atlantic

trade from São Tomé continued until the last quarter of the sixteenth century when

it suddenly went into a rapid decline. By the end of the sixteenth century, except

for slaves for the island's plantations, São Tomé was used only for ship repairs

and provisions.

Three events had caused the downturn in São Tomé's prominence: the

newly created sugar plantations in the Caribbean were much more productive, the

Kingdom of Congo was invaded twice (by the Tio in 1566-7, and by the Jaga in

1571-73) and had to be bailed out by the Portuguese military, and the Portuguese

had come to far more beneficial terms with the Ndongo to the south. In 1576, the

Portuguese shifted their attention to the newly formed post of St Paul de Luanda,

and this became the primary Portuguese shipping port to the Americas.2

1582 - Furious rivalries developed among Europeans.

Britain engaged in the race (John Hawkins carried the first cargo in 1562)

dominated the seas and take leadership of the slave trade. The methods of action

were simple:

To convince blacks that they was the first European country to chase other

slave shorelines. The Netherlands appeared and discussed the control ports of the

Congo, and Angola to the Portuguese, and villages which dared with France were

cannoned. The Englishman John Hawkins arrived in the coast of Guinea in 1562

on a ship named Jesus curiously, Raffles cargoes of other boats. It also happened

after dealing with a Negro king and buy from some captives, Hawkins went on

the king himself, his wives and his court. He became the richest merchants of

England and eventually is appointed Treasurer of the fleet and Knight, he put in

his cabinet roped a Negro, half dead.

Strategic points like Arguin, Goree, Elmina, Sao Tome and Luanda was

2 Source: "The Slave Trade", Hugh Thomas, 19

showing as the availability of slaves. What were the tools of trafficking?

It was companies at the first. European merchants congregated in the fight

against a significant risk of a trade that, in the best case, kept ships at sea for eight to ten months. In 1626, the Rouen Company (France) has asked to Richelieu

to begin on the coasts of Africa. In 1697, the French Parliament authorizes the

freedom of trade to all citizens of its territory, which triggered an extraordinary

boom, while the royal company has nine years (1680-1697). They had sent 259

vessels to load 46396 Africans, while private traders have tampers 42 000 Africans

in less than two years to Jamaica.

A very special type of monopoly law was sold by Spain to an individual or a

country to carry a given number, see a certain tonnage of Negroes in its American

colonies. It's Asiento; grants for the first time by the Flemish Charles V and which

successively passes to Genoa, Portuguese and English. The Portuguese Company

of Guinea signed the contract in 1696 and undertakes to furnish ten thousand tons

of Africans. We note that America will not be commercially surplice because of

lack of fleet. The Invincible Armada of Philip II, having been dispersed in the

large of British Islands, Portuguese never has a large shadow of ships.

Fleets are also an indispensable tool. Ships are equipped with special

equipment, horseshoes, and chains, bridges to secure and store human cargo with the least possible waste of space. Instructions of ship-owners to captains are

pieces of literature. Everything is fine-tuned, morning and evening prayers, prices

of Negroes, colic ratings and cleanliness of the pots.

Ships that launched across the Atlantic between the three continents have

made a profit every major step of this triangular trade. Ports such as Nantes,

Bordeaux, St. Malo, and Liverpool became specialized in the slave trade and built

their wealth on the ebony.

On the coast of Africa, the attachment points had nothing but the proud

splendor of European ports. Counters had the advantage of allowing a faster

turnaround in the fleet since the stock of Negroes was waiting ships. But around

these counters, local princes demanded sometimes significant rights. Brokers,

performers, grits, intermediate marinating in a broth culture were greed, cunning,

cruelty coexisted. These blacks and whites slave hunters got along very well.

Some preferred to indulge in slave trafficking improvised coastwise, they do

not have counters installed legally, but this method was longer and not without

risk, slave hunter stripped of all his possessions including his clothes do could

save his skin, unless it is paying the cost of a ritual feast. Cannibalism, as in

ancient Egypt existed in some forest areas for magical rites.

The traffic was also made by the stations, stops, counters; they were installed

in the Islands of Los, Elmina, Fernando Po and Sao Tome, etc. Luanda. English

and Dutch was strict and employed less whites but did not hesitate to install a

minimum of infrastructures. In the Island of Los, they opened the ship repair

yards and buildings.

The wood of ebony, which was the reason for this traffic? A shipment of the

Senegalese company was seized by Irish creditors gives us an idea. Seventeen

thousand hides, thirty-eight tons of gum, over a tone of ivory. Abbe Demanet

writes the "iron and brandy up the most essential part trade for Africa, provided

they have iron and brandy, it is assured treaties must necessarily all parts of the

beads is the commodity that is cheaper for the negotiations and they have more

profit. Without the beads, the colony could not continue, the Negroes, the mulatto

and mulatto women in prodigious wear belts on three or four rows of thick,

there are tissues on a red background had a considerable advantage in trafficking

captives, in the exchange that is made against the country's gold, a symbol

iron bar, earrings, fabric and clothing which were often only old clothes, Herds

colorful and old clothes theater transferred barns on the African coast, which has quite matched its functions, alcohol flowed freely was often adulterate, cutting

water, as the board of a slaver Dutch, Spanish soap added so that it comes up a

little frothing which is evidence for Negroes infallible quality"Alcohol was the

easiest way to chain the slaves for export, more dangerous than the glass beads,

guns became more and more important in the traffic, these weapons was more

dangerous to users than their opponents .

On the map, the rating is thus divided into seven sectors, Sierra Leone,

Senegal, Galam, Guinea, Cote d'Ivoire and the kingdoms of Ardres of Judah

and Benin, and finally the region of Loango and Angola. It was observed that

Congo was not on the list. Angola, which had replaced Congo, remains for several

centuries before the Gold Coast and Benin, the paradise of slavers. Each sector

also had a reputation for providing a variety of well determined slaves, rated in

certain slave-trading ports in Europe and America. Blacks slaves of Cayor are

good slaves but organized revolts. The Bambara are stupid, soft and strong. Slaves

of Gold Coast and Houidah are good farmers but easy to suicide. Congolese, are

good workers. The captive was soon called "Pieces of India," it was young black slaves from fifteen to twenty-five years without any defect with their fingers and

teeth, without a membrane in the eyes and excellent health. Also equivalence

was established. Children from three to seven years are a " one piece," a mother

and her child are "one piece." The exchange was done on a barter basis, but

ultimately conventional units of accounts were adopted in many outlets, it was

an ounce, package and bar. Each commodity was expressed as ounces. Other

currencies also was used cowries, shells, powder and grains of gold which was

also sometimes the plates, because some specialized jewelers working for the

black and white escrows.

When local authorities had given permission to open operations, trafficking

was being conducted under a routine scenario. Slaves brought from the interior or

heap along the coast was stored in unclean stores called barracoons. Around these

sinister buildings, are held scenes from hell, especially the separation of mothers

with their children.

Pruneau de POMMEGORGE, employed on the coast of Africa said: "I went

one day to a merchant, he introduced me several captives, among them, a woman of twenty to twenty four years, very sad, in pain, large breasts, which made me

suspect that she had lost her child. I did ask the merchant, he replied that she did

not. As it was forbidden to speak to this unfortunate, risk of being killed, I decided

to squeeze the tip of her breast, which came out of milk, enough to tell me that she

was breast feeding. I insisted that she has had a child; nobody cares, this should

not prevent me to buy the woman because her child would be thrown to the wolves

at the evening.

I was speechless, I was ready to retire to devote myself to my reflections on

this horrible action, but the first thing that came to mind was that I could save this

child. Accordingly, I told the seller that I would buy this woman on condition that

he delivered the child. He soon had bring me the child and I now have handed

to his mother who, not knowing how to thanks me, take earth with her hand and

threw on her forehead. Although on this occasion I did what any honest man

would have done in my place. I retired with a delicious sense, but yet mingled

with horror. As this type of crime was reiterated every day, I was obliged to refrain going among merchants because my fortune could not have enough if these good

deeds. And these are men, French men who call themselves Christians, whom

interested in committing such acts."

The view of the concentration camp triggered among blacks, few days ago,

they came and went in their native bush. Revolts brutally repressed. Pruneau

described one scene in the Island of Goree. Five hundred slaves were plotting

to massacre whites; they are betrayed by a child of twelve, put in irons for a

small theft. That child will reveal everything. Come back from work, slaves are

surrounded, enchained. The next day, they all appeared, but the lawsuit is brought

against two leaders who headed their countries. The two leaders, far from denying

the facts or seek subterfuge, they responded with courage they have to take the life

of all whites of the island, not by hatred, but they cannot oppose their flight. All

of slaves had the greatest shame of not being killed with weapons in hand on the

Battlefield for their king, but as they currently lack the time, they preferred death

to captivity.

All other captured cried in a unanimous voice "is true, is true." The board of

Whites came together to give an example to all the other captives, it was decided

That the two chief of the revolt would be put to death the day before, in front of

Captives and the population of the island.

Mr. God let me explain you about the definition of slavery:

Slavery is a system under which people are treated as properly to be bought and sold, and are forced to work, slaves can be held against their will from the times of their captive, purchase or birth and deprived of the right to leave, to refuse to work, or to demand compensation.

The Court: Ladies and gentlemen, good morning. We are ready to proceed with the closing arguments of counsel in this case. Because the government has the burden of proof in the case, you will hear first from counsel for the government. And Counsel for the defendants will have an opportunity for a rebuttal argument. Following the arguments, I will instruct you on the law.

We will take our usual recess except we'll limit the noon recess to two hours today. We want to give a full and fair opportunity to both sides to present their arguments in the case, and we'll also ask counsel to help us with timing the recesses so that we don't interrupt at a time that may be inconvenient for the lawyers making the argument. Also under the procedures here, the lawyers for both sides have an opportunity to change off, that is, not one counsel's responsible for the entire argument. They can split it up. So we're ready to proceed.

Mr. Samuel Fort (Prosecutor), you're going to present the government's case:

Mr. Samuel: I am, your honor.

May it please the Court.

ClOSING ARGUMENT

Mr. Samuel Fort (Prosecutor): Honorable Judge, Counsels, ladies and Gentlemen of the jury, good morning. After review all archives, complaint for the plaintiffs against Mr. God and Satan Lucifer, Mr. God, my question to you, since you created the earth, how many people you kill without committed a crime? You bomb the earth with storm, hurricane, earthquake, famine, disease; thousand people lost their live, million damages.

Mr. God, you had been accused in this court for non-assistance of person in danger, child molestation, rape, murder, wars, million lost live, billion damage.

I request to the jury to find Mr. God guilty and sentence him to death, he need to pay the consequences of all atrocity that he committed, without this guy, the earth will be in peace.

Mr. Satan Lucifer, you know what you are here in this court, you are a big myth in this planet, the first and the last instigator, you incite people to commit murders, wars, genocides, rape, child abuse, molestation, today will be the end of you contact with people in the earth, the only that I request to the jury, guilty verdict, and sentence you to death.

Defense lawyer Mr. Boyd Babylon: Honorable judge, ladies, gentlemen of the jury, thank you for all attention regarding this case, I'm a defense lawyer of Mr. God, you hear all accusation against my client, don't forget who this Guy, his is a loving father, the created, his is above everything . He created this world because he loves us. He gives us brain, intelligent, use what he give us, don't be stupid, think first. Let me explain about the law: Generally in a debate, when there is no proof to whether a certain thing happens or not, the logical position would be not to make assumptions about the issue and avoid using it in an argument. In this particular case, the state failed to show beyond a reasonable doubt that my client commits a crime, because state failed to proof that my client commits a crime, I recommended to the jury non guilty verdict. Thank you.

Ottom Atom, Defense lawyer for Satan Lucifer, Thank you honorable Judge, ladies, gentlemen of the Jury thank you for patience and attention in this matter, I'm a defense lawyer of Satan, his is a nice guy, love human like anybody in this planet, my client had been accuse over, over in this earth for nothing, people know the different, between good and bud, his not my client obligation to teach you the different, what? His you decision to select good and the bad, my client had nothing to do with the earth misconduct. Don't forget , Mr. God is a problem in this planet, my client had been manipulated by Mr. God many times, remember what God did about Job, God ordered Satan to destroys Job live, he did what Mr. God asked him to do, what next? Did my client is the one to blamed? No, God order Satan to do that. My client never excites people in the earth without God participation. My recommendation that my client is not guilty for any charged. Thank.

Final close argument by the State:

Mr. Samuel Fort (Prosecutor): Why does God allow natural disasters: Earthquakes, hurricanes, tsunami, cyclones, mudslides, wildfires, diseases, famine, and others natural disasters, million tragedies that cause billion death, without any explanation, Did God action is worse than a terrorists? The answer will be yes, Mr. God allow natural disasters to kill billion people over the world. The Earth know that Mr. God is present all over the planet, Woman, child, had been kill in front of God, non-assistance of person in danger, billion people had been kill in the wars, God was the only to help avoid the wars, save people live, but Mr. god never approached the killing to stop genocide, rape, child abuse, molestation. Dear Jury, my recommendation to you, fined God guilty and sentences him to death.

Presiding Judge Recommendation for deliberation to the jury:

Ladies and gentlemen of the jury, the court appreciated your patience, your attention and consideration of all arguments, archives documents for the earth.

You must decide all facts in this case; evidence received in this trial, and not from any sources credibility, believability, the evidence which you are to consider in this case consists of the testimony of the witnesses. Jury room should not be so loud that it can be heard outside the room. Until a verdict is announced, no outsider should ever know what goes on in the jury room. You should make every reasonable effort to reach a verdict, as it is desirable that there be a verdict in every case. Each of you should respect the opinions of your fellow jurors as you would have them respect yours, and in a spirit of tolerance and understanding endeavor to bring the deliberations of the whole jury to an agreement upon a verdict. Do not be afraid to change your opinion if the discussion persuades you that you should. Please don't agree to a verdict that violates the instructions of the court. Not a juror agrees to a verdict of guilty unless the juror is convinced of the defendant's guilty beyond a reasonable doubt.

Thank you again for all sacrifices you did.

References:

Amnesty International

Author: Kwame Dawes

Edwidge Danticat (Author).

William I O'neill (A democracy at war).

Thomas Howell (War Board).

Lee Kennett (War).

Bible (Job).

Arab Muslim World Architect of Slavery in Africa, Jean Marie Dia

United Nations Archives

Antony Beevor (British Historian).

Encyclopedia Britannica

Universal tribunal court has decided to take God, Satan to the court, for multiples reason: Genocide, Wars, Rape, Earthquakes (Natural disasters).

Where is God? Some have a hard time reconciling this disaster with God's goodness, while others divorce God from what they see as a natural disaster; God lets the victims grieve and lets disease spread and children suffer abuse.

The Author has been trying to figure out why God created natural disaster? Is God able to avoid Genocide, Rapes, Wars, and beheading people?

How a God who is powerfully, can be considered good and loving?

People look at the world around them and they see a lot wrong with it, Babies are born with birth defects, people are die tragically, natural disaster kill thousands of innocents, why does God create bad things?

Universal tribunal court charged God, Satan for crimes against humanity, non-assistance of person in danger.

$98.00

ISBN 978-0-692-24949-9

59800>

9 780692 249499